Everything There Was to Tell

EL LEÓN LITERARY ARTS
BERKELEY
MĀNOA BOOKS
HONOLULU

Everything There Was to Tell

BEN SCHWARTZ

El León Literary Arts
1700 Shattuck Avenue, No. 2
Berkeley, CA 94709
www.elleonliteraryarts.org

Mānoa Books
3718 Loulu Street
Honolulu, HI 96822
www.manoafoundation.org

ISBN 978-0-9891277-7-6
Library of Congress Control Number 2019910805
Printed in the United States of America
Cover design by Andrea Young
Text design by Peak Services
(www.peakserviceshawaii.com)

These stories are works of fiction. Names of characters, places, and incidents are fictitious. Resemblance to persons living or dead is coincidental. The author thanks Thomas Farber, without whom this book would not have been made, and Pat Matsueda for line editing.

Special thanks to Denny Abrams.

Photograph on title page: *Rockfish River* by Alan Mawyer.

CONTENTS

for Susan

All that I have said and done,
Now that I am old and ill,
Turns into a question till
I lie awake night after night
And never get the answers right.

What do we know but that we face
One another in this place?

"Man and the Echo," William Butler Yeats

The Man Who Killed My Dad

I

For too many years I hated the man who killed my dad.

He was living at that time in a one-bedroom rental cottage in Offenburg, a small town off Interstate 44 near the Gasconade River, fifty miles west of St. Louis. I'd come home for Christmas and was visiting overnight with my high school teacher, Gretchen, and her husband Alec. She and I maintained a friendship ten years after I took classes from her; we stayed up late discussing local politics, education, love, life, liberty, rural poverty. By the time we turned in past midnight, a storm was blowing through. Wind whined around the corners of the house, under the eaves. Squalls pounded windows and shutters intermittently. I dozed off and on until the storm subsided, then fell into deep sleep.

At 7:18 the next morning, Alec shook me awake to tell me something had happened with my dad—he didn't know what. My brother Joel was coming to pick me up in twenty minutes. He arrived in fifteen.

"What's this about?" I asked as we left for Offenburg.

"I'm not sure. I got a call from Frank Wiegers. He wouldn't tell me anything."

"Did you ask if Dad's okay?"

"I did. He wouldn't say."

"Then we have to assume the worst."

"Yes," Joel said.

We rode in silence. The highway ran along a ridge through rolling Missouri farmland. Fields green with mid-winter fescue sloped into small creek valleys. A pale white band rimmed the horizon, suspending the gray winter sky over the land.

Arriving Offenburg, we took Plassmeyer Road through town, past the water tower and grain elevators, past the farmers' feed store our dad had run for years, then across the railroad tracks to the cluster of cottages nestled between the railroad and river. Joel turned on the frontage road and stopped at the third one. Four cars were parked in the driveway.

"I don't like this," Joel said. "That's Father Rieschel's car."

"What would he be doing here?"

"What do you think he'd be doing here?"

I didn't want to think. Some of my loudest arguments with Dad were over his mindless Catholicism, arguments that had come frequently during my college years. He was heartbroken I'd lost my faith, which I really hadn't. I'd just left pieces of it lying around, and never went back to pick them up. After I graduated, our confrontations became less frequent, but dissension remained. It was good his cottage was small. I rarely stayed overnight on visits, so he no longer was able to ask the next morning, in his quiet way, "Since you're here, are you going to walk to Mass with me today, Karl?"

Good God, I hated that. Not "Are you going to Mass with me?" Not "Are you going to pray with me?" But simpler and harder not to do, "Are you going to walk to Mass with me today, Karl?" One visit I did walk with him, over the railroad tracks, up the hill, along the main street to the steps of St. Barnabas Catholic Church.

"Okay, I've walked to Mass with you," I said. "I'll see you back at the barn when it's over."

"You walked to church, son," he replied calmly. "The Mass is inside and requires attention."

He could have gone ballistic on me but didn't. So, who won that one?

A second car belonged to Frank Wiegers, who'd called Joel. A third was a county sheriff sedan backed diagonally into the driveway so it could be driven out quickly. The fourth car was Dad's 1982 Chevrolet Caprice. He'd never driven anything other than a Chevy, usually traded up every two or three years.

Joel and I walked up the driveway to the house. When we pushed the door open and came in, Father Rieschel and Frank Wiegers were sitting in front of the woodstove. They got up quickly.

"We have terrible news," Father Rieschel said, walking up to and placing his hand on Joel's shoulder. "Your dad has been called to Christ."

"Dead?" I asked. I knew damned well what he meant.

"This is Ernie's son from California, Father," Frank explained.

"Yes, the elder son," Father Rieschel said.

Joel and I sat on the two remaining chairs at the kitchen table, side by side, very close. Joel wept in huge blubbering sobs; I put my arm around his shoulders. Letting it lie there, he sat with arms cradling his stomach. It's a sad fundamental of human nature that until we're with someone we're close to when they're in great pain we don't know how much we love them. It's a sad fundamental of human experience that sometimes there's nothing we can do.

Don't know how long we sat like that, seemed like a long time. The deputy sheriff came in through the back door, the door to the yard and woodshed.

"Have you heard from the doc?" Frank asked.

"Just got out of surgery in Jefferson City. Should be here in an hour," the deputy said.

Doc Michaels was the county coroner. He managed the responsibility while handling a considerable private practice and serving as orthopedic surgeon at a Jefferson City hospital. The deputy sheriff was Roger LeClair. I'd gone to high school with him. He was two years behind me, but I remembered him from basketball. He was the most disciplined defensive player I'd ever played against. Six-three or so, he never went for a fake, never left his feet, never took his eyes off you. He was always there, on the balls of his feet, ready to move with you wherever you went. Thin, fit, he looked as if he could still play.

"Sorry about this, Joel," he said to my brother. "And you too, Karl. My deepest sympathy."

"Are you leaving him out there, Roger?" I asked.

"Yes, we can't move the body until the coroner has determined the cause of death."

"I want to see him," I said, getting up.

"I'm sorry, Karl. You can't," Roger cautioned, raising a hand to stop me. I swear I remembered the lines of his palm from having his hand in my face during basketball practice. He was standing too close to me now. I could have jab-stepped and gone around him. "Until the coroner has determined the cause of death, it's still considered a crime scene. Only authorized personnel allowed."

"That's my dad, and you're telling me I can't go out there?"

"You can't, Karl."

"I want to see him! I don't care about any fucking only authorized personnel allowed."

"Karl, stop it," Joel said.

"I don't think it's right to leave him alone out there, Joel."

"Sit down, Karl, please."

Joel's voice quavered. I wondered if he might be close to cracking. I love my brother. I sat down.

Again we waited: no one talking, no one moving. Deputy LeClair remained standing, his butt against the kitchen counter. Frank had fired the stove and it was warm in the small room. Burning wood crackled occasionally; flames licked bright orange in the stove's glass window.

Deputy LeClair left to check the radio in his patrol car. When he came back, he announced Doc Michaels had been further delayed, wouldn't arrive for at least another hour.

"Let's go to the rectory and get started with the funeral arrangements," Father Rieschel suggested.

"That's a good idea," Joel said.

"And leave Dad here alone? I don't want that," I said.

"Roger is here."

"Roger's the sheriff. I don't think we should leave Dad with Roger. We need to be with him."

"We can't go out there anyway, Karl. Roger has told us that."

"And that's bullshit. I don't care what Roger's told us."

"It's not bullshit," Roger said. "It's the law."

"It's not the law, Roger. It's the rule. I'd bet my last paycheck there's not a word in the Missouri codes anywhere that says you can't see your dead father because his body's lying in a crime scene. It's a rule you follow, Roger. That's all it is."

"Karl, don't," Joel said, pleading for me to stop.

Father Rieschel walked over and placed a hand on my shoulder. "I know this is hard for you, my son."

"I'm not your son," I said.

I lifted his hand off my shoulder. He didn't seem to mind.

"In a time of such unexpected loss, it's almost impossible not to wonder how God can let such things happen. Our best hope, however, remains our faith. We must turn to Christ, my son, to find strength and stamina to bear what has been given us. Christ will be there to solace you, I assure you."

I could see Jesus Christ waiting around to solace me. Not a busy day worldwide, He was probably hanging down at the river. Of course, omnipotent as He is, He would know I'd be coming this morning to pick up the solace He was packing. I could imagine Christ getting antsy.

"Let's get out of here," I said, and stood up. Joel stood too.

"We'll see you at the rectory, Father," Joel said.

"I'll wait here with Roger," Frank said.

"You don't have to, Frank," Roger said. "Everything is secured."

We left and got in our cars—Joel and I in his, Father Rieschel in his—and drove back across the railroad tracks and up the hill, Joel leading, Father Rieschel following, along Main Street to the rectory at St. Barnabas. A sign identifying the building as 'The Rectory' was mounted on a bracket over the lintel, and swung with a high-pitched shriek in the morning breeze. We entered a hallway where Father Rieschel took off his long winter coat and hung it on a wall hook. He gestured for us to do the same, but neither Joel nor I did.

"We do have heat here," he said. "You'll get warm in those."

"That's all right, Father. I'm fine," Joel said.

He led us through a door into his office.

"Have a seat," he said, pointing toward chairs in front of his polished L-shaped wooden desk.

The seats and backs of the chairs were cushioned and covered with a tweed fabric, dark gray—sacerdotal to a fault—the armrests wood. On one corner of the desk, a stack of books, next to an ornate crucifix with brass base. On the other corner an in-out box for letters. Open in the center of the desk a ledger. A painting of the crucifixion with Mary standing under the cross hung on the corner wall next to a bookcase with books filed neatly, large to small, on each shelf. Next to the bookcase a small fireplace with a mirror above. On the mantle a Resurrection triptych: Christ rising in vivid orange from a small grave in the center panel, two angels beating hell out of a winged serpent in the left panel, and in the right two angels reaching down from heaven to receive Christ.

Little about the arrangement seemed promising, but Joel and I sat down. Father Rieschel sat facing us. Elbows on desk, he folded his hands as if about to pray, then started speaking into them.

"I know that foremost in your minds is the concern whether your father as a suicide can be buried with the rites of Holy Mother Church."

I couldn't vouch for Joel, but if Father Rieschel was reading my mind, he'd misread. I don't think concern for whether my father could be buried with the rites of Holy Mother Church had even bought a ticket on my rapid transit of concerns.

"Suicide, of course, is a terrible and serious mortal sin. It's especially heartbreaking because it defies the love we owe God; it violates our faith in that the suicide could no longer accept, 'Thy will be done.' 'What unsurmountable anguish must fill someone,' we ask ourselves, 'to withdraw from the love of God and kill oneself?'"

He paused, fingers still poised as if to pray. Joel said nothing. The rectory sign outside shrieked in the wind. Close to screaming, I said nothing.

"I think it's important," he went on, looking up to make eye contact, "to understand your father could not have been in his right mind. We know of his struggles with depression. Our Catechism teaches us that grave psychological disturbance or anguish diminishes the responsibility of the one committing suicide. I want to assure you, your father's spiritual health was excellent. He attended daily Mass, often receiving the Eucharist; his church dues are up to date; his membership in the Sodality of Mary current. His faith was well known in our community. I don't think we're amiss to bury him with the rites of Holy Mother Church."

He paused again, and waited. I thought it Joel's responsibility to reply. It was his parish, his priest; he still attended Mass on Sundays. I didn't dare speak. Dad had been hospitalized for chronic depression twice during the last fifteen years. I didn't need a frocked pseudo-analyst to tell me he was nuts.

"So, we'll offer a funeral Mass for the repose of your father's soul and as a healing grace for all of us who grieve his loss. If there's anything special you'd like as part of the service—a homily, a eulogy by one of you, or by someone special to the family—we should probably talk about it now."

He looked at Joel, looked at me, then back at Joel.

"I don't think so," Joel said. "Is there anything you can think of, Karl?"

"I think he should be horsewhipped," I said loudly.

"Don't do this, Karl, please."

"That's what he always said when someone did something terribly wrong. That was him. The neighbor, the county commissioner, the governor. If they really fucked up, he'd say, 'They ought to be horsewhipped.' That's the way he was."

"He didn't mean anything by it, Karl. He just said that." Joel was trying hard not to weep, holding his hands over his mouth and chin.

"He was tough and mean in his way. He went to church, but he believed in retribution. If you screwed up bad, you deserved to be horsewhipped. And he screwed up bad. He killed my fucking dad!"

"He was my dad too."

"I know, Joel, I know. I loved him, Joel. I don't think he ever knew it, but I loved him."

"I loved him too, Karl. He knew," Joel said.

We sat in those chairs and wept. Father Rieschel made no move to comfort us.

II

We spent an hour at the rectory before Joel had settled everything. I was amazed at the considerations Father Rieschel brought up.

He would be able to preside at a visitation Wednesday evening but not Thursday. Would there be someone to lead the second visitation? Joel was certain someone would. Neither asked if I wanted to.

Did we have a processional hymn we'd prefer? Joel didn't, I didn't. Father Rieschel suggested "Ave Maria." I nixed it. He suggested "I Know That My Redeemer Lives." "Liveth," I said. "What?" he asked. "I Know That My Redeemer Liveth," I said. "That's Handel," he said. "'I Know That My Redeemer Lives' is a hymn." "And where does that leave Handel?" I asked.

"I don't see anything wrong with 'Ave Maria,'" Joel said.

I let it go. It was hard for me to overestimate how little I cared about these choices. Everything involved the Church, everything involved the Mass. Why should there be choices? Didn't the friggin' Roman Catholic Church have a standard prayer, a standard Mass, a standard grave, a standard clod of dirt to toss after the coffin? It would seem after two thousand years, burial with the rites of Holy Mother Church should be well established. I held my peace, listened to the rectory sign.

There was no pattern. It would shriek, be still, shriek again. I tried to imagine the physics. Gravity holds the sign at rest perpendicular to the ground. The wind blows, lifts the sign; it shrieks. The wind abates; gravity pulls the sign back. The wind again, another shriek, gravity again.

Father Rieschel asked about perpetual Mass enrollment for the deceased. To his credit, Joel didn't think we needed that yet. He'd start with two or three Masses in the next two or three months and see how things stood after that. I thought three Masses a reasonable choice. Father Rieschel added it to the funeral tab.

"And throw in a few extra bucks to fix that sign," I said.

Joel turned and looked at me, not puzzled as if he wished he knew where I was coming from, but tolerantly, as if he'd long given up on me, as if he'd expected me to say something nonsensical. The look reminded me of Dad, who had had the same habit of staring, saying nothing, as if reassuring me with his blank expression that he did not condemn the silliness of my thoughts and loved me anyway.

"Can't you hear the goddamned sign screeching?" I asked.

"Karl, must you?"

"You know I really don't notice it anymore," Father Rieshcel said. "It's windy this morning, but most of the time it's very quiet in here."

"It's not that bad, Karl," Joel said. "We're almost done here anyway."

My brother could be a strange one. He seemed incredibly calm making all the funeral arrangements, determined, sitting straight and broad-shouldered in front of Father Rieschel's desk. Twenty-five years old, powerful muscled arms lying relaxed in his lap, he seemed totally accepting of all the priestly prattle. Maybe he believed it. I hadn't the slightest idea what he believed. We'd never talked about faith. He'd spent three years in the Marines, then came back to take over the family farm. He must have believed some shit to join the Marines. I'd been drafted. Served two years as an army medic. I'd had few choices; the Marines had been asking for it.

"Stupid," I told him when he told me he'd joined. Our twin sisters were less kind.

"Very stupid," Rachel said.

"Very, very stupid," Rita said.

"We have to call our sisters," I said.

Joel and Father Rieschel turned to me and nodded.

"That's right," Father Rieschel said. "I'd forgotten Ernie had daughters too. You should call them at once. You can use my phone and office."

"Oh no, we can do that later," Joel said.

"No, no. Do it now. Go ahead."

Father Rieschel got up quickly and left the office, closing the door quietly behind him. Joel spread his open hands in a gesture of helplessness, looking at me as if I should know where to begin.

"We could start with Rita in Chicago," I said. "It's not likely she's home, but we could try."

Rita ran some kind of English-as-second-language training program at the Motorola plant in Schaumburg and did a reverse commute to Chicago. She was out early most mornings, home late. Joel reached across the desk, dragged the phone toward him, and dialed. He knew her number by heart. I could hear the phone ringing, then the answering machine.

"We can't leave a message," I said.

"I know that, Karl."

"Hey, Rita. Joel. Down here on the farm. I've got an issue I want to talk to you about. Give me a call when you can," he said, and hung up.

Okay, we could leave a message.

He pushed the phone across the desk to me.

"You do Rachel," he said.

"It's 6 a.m. in Hawai'i. You want to wake her?"

Joel shrugged; I dialed. The phone rang several times, but no one answered. Rachel was married to an anesthesiologist. They should be used to getting calls at all hours. The phone switched to an answering machine, then Rachel came on. "Hold on, hold on, while I shush this thing," she said. I waited; the machine stopped.

"Hello," I said.

"Is that you, Karl?"

"Yes."

"Jesus Christ, Karl, are you in Berkeley? You know damned well it's six in the morning in Hawai'i. Why in God's name do you want to wake me?"

"Dad's dead," I said.

"Oh," she said.

"He hanged himself. They found him in the woodshed."

Rachel didn't say anything. I waited. Joel reached for the phone.

"We know you might not be able to come," he said. "We'll delay the funeral as long as we can. You were out here just two weeks ago, and the boys have to be taken care of and Greg has to be on call, so we understand if you can't come."

There was another long pause from her end of the line.

"Hello, Rachel," Joel said.

"I'll have to get back to you, Joel," Rachel said. She hung up.

I thought it strange Joel assured her she didn't have to come. Jesus Christ, they had enough money to buy a private jet and fly it out if they wanted. I didn't see any reason in the world why Rachel couldn't come.

"I bet she's not coming," I said.

"We don't know that, Karl. Let's not assume anything."

I liked Rachel; I hoped she would come. Rita I could take or leave. After our mother died of cancer years before, Rita appointed herself matriarch, assigned herself a mother's role of never being satisfied with her children. Her criticisms were harsh and, unfortunately for me, far too accurate. She made it clear my hobbling along as a job-shopping proposal writer did not meet her expectations. Why she was entitled to expectations was never discussed. She had a soft spot in her heart for Joel since he had been the youngest when Mom died. And that he was doing much better than his older brother, in her estimation, seemed to gratify her enormously. That it seemed to gratify her needled me, and she knew it. I think she believed that irritation would spur me to some achievement she could approve of. I didn't care that much about her approval, but she was the older sis—seven minutes before Rachel, years before Joel and me—and deserved credit for holding the four of us together since she was a teenager. There was no doubt Rita would come to the funeral, though Rachel, if she came, might arrive first since she'd be flying in from Hawai'i. Rita would be driving from Chicago. It wasn't complicated; the logistics were just difficult.

Father Rieschel and Joel set the funeral for Friday, as far as they could push it according to Father Rieschel, since he didn't do funerals, he said, on weekends.

"Do you go over that with your parishioners before they die?" I thought of asking, but held my peace.

We were finished in the rectory. Joel thought it best to check back at Dad's. Frank's car was still in the driveway but everyone else was gone. We parked and went into the house, which was empty, the back door open though it was January in the Midwest. I walked toward the open door.

"I'm not sure I want to go out there," Joel said.

"I'm sure I do," I said, and went out and crossed the yard.

The woodshed door was also open.

Frank was sweeping sawdust across a wet spot in the open space between the workbench and woodpile. "I thought I'd clean up. Ernie liked to keep things neat, you know," he said.

Firewood was stacked in two even ricks against one wall of the shed, segregated by size in each rick, larger blocks in the back one, smaller split pieces in the front. Hanging above the workbench bolted into the opposite wall were multiple tools, each outlined with a black marking pen. I took the small short-handled flat shovel from its outline and held it on the floor for Frank to sweep up the sawdust. The dark wet spot remained.

Three feet of braided polyester cord dangled from a rafter above the spot, the end of the cord attached with a clove hitch.

"I'm sorry I didn't take that down," Frank said.

"Why? That's what he did it with, right?"

"Yes," Frank said.

Joel stood in the doorway, but didn't come in. I placed the shovel back in its outline above the work bench and took down a double-bitted axe.

"What are you doing, Karl?" Joel asked.

"I'm cutting that down."

"Do you have to?"

"Yes, I have to," I said.

Joel turned and disappeared. I didn't know why he'd want to leave the rope up. I didn't know why he decided not to watch. I severed the knot with one blow—Dad's tools were always sharp. The cord dropped; I caught it before it hit the floor.

"Are you going to keep that?" Frank asked.

"Yes. What happened to the rest of it?"

"They took it with them."

"It was still around his neck?"

"Yes," he said very softly.

"It's all right, Frank. I want to know what happened. It doesn't make it any worse to know."

"I don't think it's important," Frank said.

"I do."

I hung the axe against its outline, then coiled the rope and stuffed it in my jacket pocket.

"He must have stood on something, Frank. Do you know what?"

Frank stared at me blankly as if he were thinking about not answering any more of my questions.

"Was it a block of wood?"

Frank didn't answer. A large round block was lying on the split pieces of the front rick. I pointed to it.

"That one?"

Frank nodded. I took the piece down. It was maybe eighteen inches long, eight to ten inches in diameter. Hard to stand on it with two feet, I thought. I set it on the chopping block and took a splitting axe off its hook. With the first blow, I split it into two even sections.

"What're you doing?" Frank asked.

"We're not going to have a fire here anymore, Frank. I want you to take this home and burn it."

"I have a large firebox. Splitting it once is enough."

"No, Frank. I want it to burn fast, I want it to burn hot and fast, I want it to burn hot and fast and quick. Throw it all in at once and let 'er roar."

I split the whole block into kindling, two-inch-diameter pieces, one-inch, half-inch, as thin as I could without splintering anything. Frank stood by watching until the block was destroyed, pieces scattered in front of me in a semi-circle. I hung the splitting axe on the wall and started to gather the kindling. Frank began to help.

"Let me get it, please."

And Frank did. He waited until I had all the pieces cradled in my arms, then walked with me to his car and opened the trunk. I tossed the kindling in.

"I'll make sure I burn it tonight," Frank said.

When we went back in the house, Joel was sitting at the kitchen table, a stack of Dad's papers spread in front of him.

"I need to go," Frank said, "unless you boys need me for something."

"Thanks, Frank. Thanks so much," Joel said.

I expected Joel to get up and hug Frank, but he just laid down the note he'd been reading and looked up at him. Frank nodded, then left.

"We've got some stuff to take care of, Karl," Joel said. "We've got some shit to get through here."

I expected him to say we had to stay on mission, but he didn't.

III

Rachel did come. The next day, Tuesday, a flight from Hawai'i arriving St. Louis 6:15 p.m. Rita wanted to coordinate driving in from Chicago with picking up Rachel, but couldn't leave Schaumburg until 3 p.m. and would be late to the airport. Rachel said she didn't mind waiting, but Joel insisted he'd be there to meet her. Rita called that silly, but Joel didn't budge. I stayed out of it. Joel asked me to ride with him. I begged off. He left for the airport early afternoon; I was free to wander around on my own.

Joel was living with Uncle Harry and Aunt Bev, who owned the farm next to Dad's, so I stayed with them too. As soon as Joel left, I put on my boots and headed for the old homestead where we'd lived as children. I climbed the boundary fence below Uncle Harry's house and walked through the pasture toward the small creek at the bottom of the hill. Vegetation was sparse, stripped by grazing. In early winter, Joel had moved the cattle to the lush fields along the river; the pasture gate had been left open. I followed the farm road into the creek crossing. There was little water. Rain from Sunday night had drained to the river; a flow of only two-to-three inches trickled over rocks and sticks, occasionally forming a small pool or eddy. A rim of thin ice had formed on each pool. As kids we broke off pieces of ice like this and let it melt in our mouths. We called it ice brittle, eating it as a substitute for peanut brittle we didn't have. Breaking off a piece, I considered a bite. The ice was thin and clear, veined with a few freeze lines. Tempting, but formed in a watershed with tons of cow manure. We hadn't considered that as children. Maybe there had been fewer cows, less manure, less urine. Maybe not.

Without tasting it, I floated my *ice brittle* sliver down the current and climbed the hill toward the house.

The doors were locked, and Joel had nailed plywood sheets over windows on the first and second stories. Why tempt some young man with a hunting rifle? The screened porch at the back was open, but nothing was there except a few empty feed sacks, a bucket of baler twine, two pairs of old work gloves. I didn't think they were Joel's. He didn't wear work gloves; his hands were hard as plowshares. Maybe they were Dad's, though I couldn't remember his ever wearing work gloves either. When we were kids, the cream separator was on the screened porch. By the summer our mom died—I was ten—one of my nightly chores was to crank through all milk to separate the cream. Dad would take apart the separator and wash it because, he said, he couldn't risk my not getting it clean and spoiling a batch of cream. I was fine with that and thought it an excellent example of his making good decisions. How could a man with the good sense to not let a ten-year old clean the cream separator not have sense enough not to kill himself?

I walked around to the front porch. It was empty, but when we lived here, it had two Adirondack chairs facing the river and the bottom fields. The summer after Mom died, Dad would sit in the darkness far into the night, chain smoking cigarettes he rolled from a tin of Velvet Pipe & Cigarette Tobacco.

Rita would come downstairs when she was ready for bed and go outside and tell him—How old was she? Thirteen?—"Dad, you need to go to bed."

Dad would say, "Thank you, Rita. As soon as I finish this smoke."

Rita would go to bed, but Dad wouldn't. He'd finish that smoke, roll and light another, and smoke that one too, until all of us were asleep, even Rita, and no one knew how long he stayed there.

I sat on the front steps and looked down toward the river. The afternoon was cold and hazy, gray—thin sunlight sifting through a partial overcast. Most of the fields were brown and dormant, or fallow, except for the fescue pastures in the bottomlands where cattle were grazing. It hadn't looked quite like this when we lived here. The pasture to the left of the house had been neglected, overgrown with oak sprouts and blackberry bushes. The woodlot to the right that Joel had completely clear-cut used to extend halfway to the river and blocked the view. So, what was there for Dad to see? What was he looking for those nights he sat here and smoked?

"Rita was right. You should have got up and gone to bed," I told him. "You shouldn't have spent so much time alone. You should have learned to talk to people instead of brooding on your sorrows, then going off to church to pray about them.

"Then to hang yourself. How could it be that bad? We had Christmas dinner together, Dad. Rachel was there. Rachel is easy to talk to. You could have said something. But no, no, that was not Ernie's way. Ernie would rather go to Mass and pray about it, rather hang himself, wouldn't he? What were you thinking anyway?

"You had to take the rope out of its special place on the wall, didn't you? Why didn't taking it down and leaving everything else in place bother you? You drew all those outlines, hung all those tools. It makes no sense, Dad. Makes no sense. How could you?"

I caught myself and stopped. I was talking to a ghost, I was talking to a memory, I was talking to a dead man, but I was also talking to the man who did it. I wanted the perpetrator challenged and interrogated, held accountable for his killing and, if guilty, sentenced. "Horsewhipped," was what I kept thinking.

I fingered the rope in my coat pocket, took it out, snapped it in the air thinking you could horsewhip someone with it. I tied a huge stopper knot in one end and pounded the rope against the step below me.

"You're damned straight, you could be horsewhipped with your own damned hanging rope, Ernie Schroeder!"

There was no one around. I could yell until my lungs burst. I untied the knot, recoiled the rope, put it back in my pocket.

After sitting on the steps awhile, I walked toward the river, cutting across the knoll below the house, angling toward the creek. It had been straightened by Joel as it dropped toward the river and served as a boundary between pasture and woodlot. I followed the fence along the bank using tractor tracks as a path. Each cow in a herd grazing to my left raised her head and stared. I reached the river, stood on the bank above it.

The water was high from the storm two nights before and flowed bank to bank, covering the gravel bars and plants usually exposed in this wide, shallow section. Bare willow branches bobbed in the edges of the light brown current, small icicles hanging from some tips. It wasn't a large river—fifteen, twenty feet wide, less than a foot deep in the shallows—but it had created this rich black soil our ancestors bought a hundred fifty years ago, when they first arrived from Germany, dark loam fields where year after year they planted corn, wheat, sometimes soybeans. Since Joel had taken over the farm, he didn't crop much. He'd turned these bottomlands into hayfields from which he harvested bales in summer. Late growth he used for winter pasture.

When we were growing up, Dad planted corn or wheat here, his cash crops, more often corn. One hot afternoon almost a year after Mom died, probably July, Dad was cultivating corn in a fifteen-acre plot along the river. Rita had baked bread. She made a cucumber-tomato sandwich, put it in a small paper bag, and told me to take it to Dad for a treat. I'd delivered the sandwich along the route I'd come today. Dad had cultivated about half the corn—the dirt was freshly turned; birds were darting after grubs and worms—but had stopped. The cultivators were in the earth, the old John Deere B tractor idling noisily. Dad was slumped in the seat, hands on the steering wheel, eyes focused on the tractor's hood as if trying to see into the green paint.

"What are you doing, Dad?" I asked, thinking I might startle him by speaking.

He turned, taking a moment it seemed to focus on me, then throttled back the John Deere.

"Karl, what are you doing here?" He sat up straight. "Is something wrong?"

"I brought you a sandwich. Rita made it." I held it up to him.

"But everything's okay?"

"Yes," I said.

He took the sandwich and ate it slowly; I had the strange thought he couldn't taste it. As he ate, he kept staring at the tractor hood but didn't say anything.

After a while, I asked, "Is the tractor okay?"

He turned to me with a sudden twist of his head, pursed his lips.

"Yes, I think the tractor's okay."

"Then why did you stop cultivating?"

"I don't know, Son. I really don't know."

"Shouldn't you be at it again?"

"Yes, I really should. I don't know why I stopped."

He throttled up the John Deere, shifted into gear, and started along the row. The cultivator sweeps turned the black soil in shallow windrows. The corn was high and bent under the tractor, popping up again when the cultivator had passed. I watched him plow to the end of the row, turn, and start along the next. I waved to him; he didn't wave back. I walked back home. Not long after, he went away for four months to a mental hospital where he was treated for anxiety and depression. Uncle Harry and Aunt Bev took us in while he was gone. They had three bedrooms upstairs.

The river had backed water into the creek for twenty or thirty yards. I retraced my steps along the fence until I could cross and walk upriver. Because most trees this side had been removed and a hayfield went nearly to the bank, I could walk easily in the stubble of mown alfalfa.

The afternoon was cold, but there was no wind. After a half hour, I cut across the bottom fields to the county road, and turned east toward Uncle Harry's house. The graveled track ran parallel to the fields for a few hundred yards, then curved to climb the hill out of the bottoms, the roadbed cutting into limestone as it topped the ridge. Three crows were feeding on a dead squirrel on the rocky crest and eyed me warily as I approached, pacing nervously, lifting wings as if about to take flight. So as not to disturb them, I stopped, sat on a boulder, and waited. The boulder was cold. I slipped the bottom of my winter coat under me.

I sat still while the crows got used to my being there. One stood sentinel for three or four minutes, then all three went back to tearing meat off the roadkill. Occasionally, pulling at a sinew that wouldn't tear, a crow would shake the squirrel from side to side, lose its grip, and send the carcass sailing through the air a few feet. All three would leap up and caw loudly, before settling down around the carcass. After a while, appearing to have forgotten me, they hopped around, pecking, in their feasting even tossing the squirrel toward me once or twice. I imagined them gorging until they couldn't fly.

A car came along the road from upriver. The crows listened as I did: the distant rip of rubber thread off packed dirt and rock, the occasional ping of gravel spun against a fender, the purr of a motor. They flapped their wings, lifted, dropped again, cawing across the carcass as if debating whether they could carry it away before the automobile reached them. I thought of getting up, getting off the road. I didn't much want to talk to anyone, and surely whoever was coming would know me, or Uncle Harry, or Joel, recognize me as part of the family, and stop. The automobile came up the hill. The birds rose with raucous cries and flew away. I didn't move.

The driver was Chris Kohler, who knew me and would definitely stop. It was almost as if he'd foreseen I'd be sitting on the rock at the top of the hill; he was slowing down long before he could have recognized me. I'd known Chris all my life. He'd owned the farm next to ours for thirty years or more. One of the times when Dad was gone for treatment, I'd stayed with Chris and his wife, Clara, for a few weeks. The river flooded that spring, flattening the fence between our farm and his, piling logs, debris, and mud in the fencerow. Uncle Harry and Chris decided I should clear it from the ridge line to the river, at least a quarter-mile. Fourteen years old, I spent three weeks cutting up logs, untangling them from barbed wire, dragging them out and stacking them in huge piles that I burned. I had an axe, a mattock, and a chainsaw. Cutting brush that had invaded the fencerow, I burned that too. I loosened barbed wire from fenceposts and burned all broken ones. I killed three copperheads before I'd finished and threw them on the fire. They sizzled in the flames and red coals.

In addition to farming, Chris worked as a section hand on the Rock Island railroad. Every afternoon about five, he'd come home and walk down to the field to critique my work. He liked that I was doing a thorough job. Though he hadn't expected it would take so long, he understood it was nasty work. He used a shovel and tamping bar every day, knew the limits of hand labor. Some evenings we'd hike to the river, strip, and dive in for a wash and swim. We were always dirty or at least I was. You can't dig logs and fenceposts out of mud and look like an altar boy. After bathing we'd go to the house for supper. Later I'd climb into the loft and fall asleep on a cornhusk mattress. At the time I thought it three of the best weeks of my life. I had work, great food, and Chris treated me as an equal even though he was fifteen years older.

He pulled his pickup to the roadside, stopping ten feet from where I was sitting, and got out. Standing next to me, he nodded a greeting, then said nothing for two or three minutes.

"Hello, Chris." I broke the silence finally.

"How you doing, Karl. You all right?"

"Yeah."

"I'm really sorry about your dad. I'm still having a hard time believing it."

"Really pisses you off, doesn't it?"

"Not really, Karl. What are you saying?"

"I'm saying he was a complete asshole to do it. It pisses me off and, if he thought I was going to bend over and feel sorry for him, he sure as shit read me wrong."

"Jeez, Karl, go easy. I'm sorry you feel that way."

"I'm not. How could he do that to himself?"

"Your dad went through a lot of shit. Your mom dying when you were just kids, paying off those medical bills, no one to run the house, trying to make a living just farming. He went through a lot."

"That was years ago. Now he had the farm paid for. He had a job. He had grown children who take care of themselves. Holy Christ, Rachel is even married to an anesthesiologist. He got through all that shit, then killed himself when the going was decent, when he had friends, neighbors, grown children he could have talked to. That's bullshit, Chris, and I'm pissed."

"There's no point to being pissed, Karl," Chris said—angrily, I thought.

"My own dad killed someone I loved. I don't forgive him."

"I don't think you should blame him that much. I'm just sorry he's gone."

"I'm sorry he's gone too, but I'm pissed he offed himself."

"I think that's wrong, Karl. I can't see any point in being mad at your dad."

"Well, I am. Who are you to say it's wrong?"

"Because I know, and I'm saying."

I didn't see any reason to quarrel with Chris. I liked him. He rocked on his heels, hands thrust deep in his coat pockets, but said nothing more. Chris too, I was sure, was grieved by Dad's suicide, probably as mystified as I about why, but processing it differently.

"I'm sorry, Chris."

"It's okay, Karl. It's a tough time for you."

He dug with the toe of his boot at the roadside gravel.

"Come on," he said. "It's cold out here. Get in the pickup. I'll run you home."

"Thanks, Chris. I want to walk. It's not far, and I'm out here to walk."

"It's warm in the pickup."

"I'm not that cold."

"Okay," he said.

Hands in pockets, he crossed the edges of his jacket so they overlapped, strolled to his pickup, and drove away.

I had lied. I was freezing, but I wanted to get rid of Chris. Who was he to tell me what I should feel? Maybe he wasn't pissed, maybe hammering railroad spikes all your life took care of your anger, but I sure as hell didn't need to hear from Chris Kohler I was out of line.

I'd thought to stay until the crows came back, but it was too cold. I got up and started toward Uncle Harry and Aunt Bev's house. Tires had worn grooves to bare rock where the road topped the bald hill. The squirrel the crows had been feeding on lay spread on white limestone like an offering on an altar. The track of Chris's truck went around the carcass; he'd swerved to miss it. The crows had picked out the eyes and torn the flesh from lips and mouth. The incisor teeth, yellow and scarred, thrust straight up from the broken and flattened face.

IV

Joel and Rachel got back from the airport at nine Tuesday night. Rita rolled in at eleven. All four of us were staying with Uncle Harry and Aunt Bev. Wednesday afternoon we went to the funeral home in Offenburg to make final arrangements with the mortician. It seemed arrangements were a big part of getting a body buried. You can't just carry it out in a field, shove it down in the dirt, and cover it. I was told we needed to pick a coffin, decide on a guest book to be used for the viewing, probably choose a wreath or two.

We drove by Dad's cottage to pick out a shirt, tie, and jacket for him to be buried in. Rita and Rachel spent a long time deciding which jacket—he only had two—and which tie—he had a dozen. I thought the St. Louis Browns baseball tie someone had given him years ago —the team had been gone from St. Louis for decades, but he still had the tie—would be excellent, but Rita nixed it.

At the funeral home, we were ushered into the chapel where the casket would be open for viewing. The mortician motioned for us to sit in the front row of chairs.

"Is he here?" I asked.

"Yes, he's here," the mortician said.

"I want to see him."

"He doesn't look that good yet. I haven't finished."

It sounded as if he were rebuilding Dad out of modeling clay or fiberglass. He'd had the body almost forty-eight hours, could have totally reconstructed it by now.

"I don't care. I want to see him."

The mortician stared at me, glanced at Rita, at Rachel, at Joel. Rachel shrugged. I stood up ready to go.

"Okay," the mortician said. "Is everyone coming?"

"No," Joel said.

"I'm staying with Joel," Rachel said.

"I'm going with Karl," Rita said.

The mortician led us down a hallway, past coffins displayed on gurneys along the wall, some with lids open, some closed. There were no cadavers in the open coffins.

"Any dead meat in those closed boxes?" I asked the mortician.

"Indeed not," he said.

"Really, Karl," Rita said.

The room he led us into was insulated, no windows, cold. The door closed behind us without a sound. A body covered with a white sheet lay on a stainless steel gurney. I walked over and pulled the sheet back. The mortician had done a lot to clean him up, but it was Dad. Face ashen, eyes closed, hair washed and combed, cheeks and neck clean shaven, mouth partially open, lips slightly parted. His tongue looked black, though it was probably just shadowed by his lips. There was an inch-wide red ring around his neck and under his left ear. Rope burn, I assumed. Reaching out, I touched the ring. There were scratches along the neck, as if Dad's fingernails might have torn at the rope as he was strangling. Rita began to cry in spite of her efforts to hold back tears.

"I'll cover that with his shirt collar," the mortician said. "He'll be wearing a tie for the visitation and viewing."

"Why cover it? Everyone who comes will know he hanged himself," I said.

The mortician looked hard at me but didn't say anything. He glanced at Rita, then back at me.

"We'll have him in the white shirt and the suit jacket you brought. None of that will show."

"Let it show," I said. I was getting loud but couldn't stop myself. "They say capital punishment deters crime, so let them see what a hanged neck looks like. Maybe we can cut the suicide rate around here. Let's get something out of this madness."

"Karl, please," Rita whispered.

"I have the rope he did it with," I said. I reached in my coat pocket and took it out. "Let's just lay this in the coffin next to his face, right along the neck there so everyone can see it. There is no reason to sanitize this shit!" I started to lay the rope next to Dad's face.

"Give me that," Rita said. She reached for the rope.

"No," I said.

"Give it to me!"

"No."

I coiled the rope and put it back in my pocket. Rita was hanging onto my arm, and now I was crying with her. We stood there holding each other, looking at Dad. It seemed so unnecessary he should be dead. I couldn't imagine what he'd been thinking at the time he offed himself and, looking down at him, I couldn't imagine his brain not thinking anymore. There was nothing wrong with him: broad face, thick forehead, everything in place. His brain was probably not damaged. Okay, he couldn't see anymore, couldn't hear anymore, couldn't talk anymore, but his brain might still be thinking like hell inside that thick skull of his.

"Stupid, Dad. Really stupid," I said.

"Karl."

"I can't help it, Rita. I can't believe he did this."

"Cover him, please," she said to the mortician.

He did, and we went out of the room and rejoined Joel and Rachel in the chapel. Neither asked about Dad. I suppose if they'd wanted to know anything, they'd have gone with us.

V

A crowd gathered for the first night's visitation. We were a large family and had cousins in every slough and silo around Offenburg. In addition, eighty percent of St. Barnabas parish practiced a rudimentary Catholicism: they made Mass on Sunday, made Reconciliation during Easter week, took Holy Communion on Easter Sunday, and showed up to pray a rosary for any parishioner laid out for visitation. This was the night Father Rieschel would lead the rosary, which added cachet to the evening. It always seemed to me Catholics, or at least the Catholics around Offenburg, believed the divine ear was more attuned if a priest was leading the muttering. It was hard to tell if they'd come out for the priest or Dad.

Men and women who did business with him at the feed store he'd run for fifteen years also came: farmers who bought fertilizers, seeds, and pesticides; livestockmen who bought hay, grain, and stock tanks; gardeners who bought pots, planters, and seed-starter kits. Most of them knew Joel and talked with him before they moved along to shake hands with Rita, Rachel, and me, to offer us their sympathy.

A short ruddy-faced man walked up to the casket, stopped to talk to Joel, then came toward us, bending over the row of chairs to offer Rachel his condolences. He looked at Rita and me. I stood and shook his hand. I could smell whiskey on him.

"And this is your lovely wife, I suppose?" he asked, leaning toward Rita.

"Oh no," I said. "This is Mother Rita."

Rita was up like a bottle rocket.

"Their sister Rita. We're all Ernie's children," she said, reaching out and shaking his hand.

"I know Joel," he said apologetically, "but not the rest of you. Ernie never talked about you very much."

"We've been gone a long time," Rita said.

"Out of sight, out of mind," I said, nodding to the speaker.

He stared at me as if he didn't understand what I'd said, then surprised us by taking the seat next to mine. He sat shaking his head, started to talk.

"I can't believe it. I walk in here, and I look at him lying there in the coffin, and I think he was alive just Saturday. He brought a load of feed out to my place, and he was just the way he always was. He didn't say anything; you know, he never talked a lot. He seemed as normal as normal could be. And now, there he is. I can't get used to it. I can't imagine why he'd do it."

"Because he was stupid," I said. Rita slammed an elbow into my ribs.

"Oh no, Ernie was smart. He was really smart. You could ask about your bill and he'd know it without even looking it up and tell you what it was, and then he'd find the bill and give it to you, and you'd look at it and there it was, exactly what he said it was. Ernie was smart, I know he was smart. He didn't do it because he was stupid."

"Maybe he did it because he was lazy. He took the easy way out." I got another shot to the ribs from Rita.

"Ernie was not lazy. I know that for sure. Saturday, he stayed and helped me carry that whole truckload of feed back to the granary. I use that old barn where we closed the hall and turned it into a machine shop, since we don't put hay in there anymore, but the granary is still in the back of the barn, and he helped me carry every sack of that feed. He didn't have to do that, but that was Ernie. He didn't mind helping. He sure wasn't lazy, and you shouldn't be saying that."

Again, here I was being told what I shouldn't be saying or shouldn't be feeling. It seemed preposterous to me no one else seemed bothered that Dad had done something devastating that hadn't needed to happen. He'd killed a man, a man not only I, but apparently all these people, loved and respected. Why was no one outraged? Did they think outrage and grief were mutually exclusive? I couldn't understand these people, I couldn't understand Dad. He'd been one of them. I wasn't.

"I suppose we'll never know," the man said, sniffling. "He was such a good man, such a good man. I just can't figure it out."

He slapped his palms hard on his knees and turned to me.

"My sympathy," he said.

"Thank you," I said.

When he left, Rita grabbed me.

"I need to talk to you," she said.

"You *need* to talk to me? I think you mean you *want* to talk to me, Rita."

"Whatever," she said, tightening her grip on my elbow.

I pushed her hand away. We marched out into the hall behind the crowded room full of people waiting for the priest to arrive, the visitation to finish.

"It's not about you," Rita said, turning to me, jabbing a finger in my face. "It's not all about you, Karl."

"Jesus Christ, Rita, flog me with a platitude. For God's sake, you can do better than that."

She was enraged, and enraged she looked exactly like Dad. She got in my face like skunk spray in an open window. If Dad had had half her *cojones,* he wouldn't be lying dead, a suicide, in the room behind us.

"Screw you, Karl. I mean it. Cut the shit! Nobody needs it. And it really isn't about you, Karl. It really isn't."

I hated those buzzwords. I'd promised myself I'd throttle anyone who ever used them with me, but I couldn't very well strangle Rita there in the hallway of the funeral home.

"Okay," I said.

"Good," she said.

She put her arm in mine, steered me back into the room, and we sat through an intoning of the rosary. "Hail Mary, Hail Mary, Hail Mary." I wanted to shout, "Hail Rita, Hail Rita, Hail Rita," but held my peace. I didn't want to risk getting led out into the hall again. So I prayed to myself, "Blessed art thou among women, Rita. Blessed art thou!" If anyone needed a prayer, she did.

VI

I was wrong about the St. Barnabas Catholics coming Wednesday night mainly to pray with the priest. The visitation room was as crowded Thursday evening with no Father Rieschel. Nothing special had been planned. Someone had suggested Uncle Harry lead the second night's rosary, and though he wasn't excited about doing it, he agreed

There was a natural sweetness to Uncle Harry. He had a hard time saying no to anyone directly, and I can't remember his ever speaking ill of anyone. He had a richly self-nourished and abiding love for his family: wife, sons, sister, nieces, nephews, and brother-in-law Ernie. He had loved his sister, our mother, with an older brother's devotion and grieved keenly when she died. He visited our dad often after she was gone—their farms were adjacent, within walking distance—perhaps hoping to share his grief. But their griefs were different, which neither could articulate; what might have bonded them, in time appeared to alienate them. A year after our mother's death, Uncle Harry and Dad rarely visited. They seemed to avoid each other and met only at family functions. Many times Harry told me Dad was never the same after our mother died, which seemed to paper over that he had lost a sister and Dad a wife but had not been able to share their sorrow. I was not surprised when Harry, sitting next to me in the family row at the second night's visitation, again brought up Dad's having changed.

"He was never the same after your mother died."

"I know, Harry. You've told me that many times."

"Well it's true: he was never the same."

"How not the same, Harry? Less honest? Less trustworthy? Less dependable?"

"No."

"He'd lost his mojo? Couldn't get around on the fastball anymore?"

"You know that's not what I'm talking about."

"Then what are you talking about? I need to know. How was he 'never the same'?"

"He never got over it. He was hurt in a way he could not heal himself."

Though I hated being pissed at Harry, I was tired of everyone cutting Dad slack. Maybe he couldn't heal himself, but he sure knew how to hurt himself, didn't he? How often were we going to play the card that a death twenty years ago justified a suicide? I didn't intend to buy that, any more than I intended to accept the puzzled shaking heads marveling that he'd done it, mystified about why he had, yet forgiving.

I hated too the way visitors drifted by the coffin, paused to look at Dad for however long, then came down the family receiving line to tell us how natural he looked. He didn't look natural, he looked dead; yet not a single mourner came by to tell us, "He really looks dead, doesn't he?" Not on your life! They said, "He looks so peaceful" or "He looks as if he's just fallen asleep," when everyone knew he had not. Jesus Christ, he'd died jerking at the end of a rope! Everything about the way the mortician presented him encouraged us to forget that. Dad's head lay on a white pillow, cheeks rouged, lips brightened with a trace of color, work-hardened hands folded across his lower chest with a rosary wrapped around them, cross conspicuously aligned with his fingers. That got me! I'm sure he'd have wanted it that way, but I wanted to rip that rosary out of his hands, open the palms so everyone could see the scars and calluses of a working man, a man of flesh and blood here on this earth, not some sanctified stooge supposedly on his way to eternal life.

"You ended it!" I wanted to yell. "It's over now, Dad. Over. You'll rot now. No one will come to raise you up. Your only ascension will be a few whiffs of carbon dioxide rising from the worms who eat you."

And I wanted to yell to everyone at the visitation, "Do you think his looking good is going to help him! Do you think the lip color, the rouge, the makeup change anything? Or the rosary around his hands? Get rid of the goddamn rosary. Look at those hands. They're human mitts; they'll turn to dust. The rosary won't change that!"

Of course I didn't say anything. I shook every hand stretched out to me, accepted every condolence offered, prided myself on how well-behaved I could be. This too would pass. "How chastening in the hour of pride! How consoling in the depths of affliction!" Abraham Lincoln had said.

When it was time to pray the rosary—which would wrap up the evening—and Uncle Harry stood to get started, Rita motioned him back down. She wanted to say a few words first. She'd taken notes and held a small sheet of yellow paper. Walking up to the coffin, she stood looking at Dad a long moment, then turned toward the people who'd come that night. All seats were taken, and some visitors were standing in the back or in the hallway. The front door was open; you could hear the occasional car go by in the distance.

"I know many of you are troubled that you did not do enough," she said. "You've told us stories about how you knew our dad and how you valued his friendship, and we thank you for those stories. And some of you have told us you wished you had taken the time to visit with him longer, or had asked more questions about how he was doing, or had stayed longer with him after church or in the store, or had invited him in for coffee when he made a delivery to your farm, that maybe all that might have made a difference. We don't know what might have made a difference; we don't know why he did what he did. But I want you to know that you did enough, that everyone here who knew our dad, who befriended him, who lived with him in the same church and the same community, and who have come here tonight to remember him, did enough. All of us are parts of each other's lives. That's all we can be: just parts. We never know completely what drives the whole. We share our lives, as you shared yours with Dad, but each life is separate and solitary; we cannot blame ourselves for the decisions made in that solitude. What each of you gave in your friendship with Dad was what you could give, and what you could give was enough."

She turned then toward the coffin and spoke to Dad.

"And I want you to know too, Dad, what you gave was enough. I wish you could see the people who have come to visit you; I wish you were alive to receive them. I wish their friendship and care could have saved you, but I want you to know your life, and the way you lived it, were enough to bring forth the affection of these people, your friends and neighbors.

And I know too you often felt you didn't do enough for us, your children; that you missed critical parts of our lives when you couldn't be with us, that you were too troubled to give what we needed when you were with us. I want you to know what you gave was enough. We have children and homes of our own. We're okay. We're more than okay. You did enough, Dad. You gave enough. We love you. We'll miss you."

She stopped and turned to us, tears streaming down her face. No one knew if she had more to say. She opened and closed her hands as if trying to explain she didn't know what to do next. Rachel went to her, hugged her, and led her back to their chairs, where they sat and held each other. A lot of noses were blown. Otherwise the room remained quiet. Uncle Harry, who was supposed to lead the rosary, remained in his chair, sobbing quietly, face in his hands. Joel stood and tapped me on the shoulder.

"Let's go," he said.

I knew what he intended. I stood up and crossed those three or four steps to the kneeler in front of the coffin, knelt with him, and together we led the rosary, the Sorrowful Mysteries: The Agony in the Garden, The Scourging at the Pillar, The Crowning with Thorns. A small prayer pamphlet in a holder by the kneeler listed them. Joel knew them by heart. A mystery, an Our Father, Hail Marys. "Blessed is the fruit of thy womb, Jesus." Then The Carrying of the Cross and, at last, The Crucifixion.

There was nothing mysterious in the sorrowful mysteries. They ended in death. There was nothing of resurrection in what we prayed that night.

VII

The day of the funeral we went first to the funeral home to say our last farewells to Dad before the mortician closed the coffin. I had no intention of saying a last farewell. I had a lot of crap to go over with Dad yet, and I fully intended for him to hear it all. Whatever hearing means to the dead. Jesus Christ, it's hard to find the right words for these things. Every thought, every concept, every idea has an euphemism, such as the mortician's referring to the body in the coffin as Dad's mortal remains. Had he hidden away his immortal remains somewhere in a back room? Why didn't he bring them out and get them in the coffin with these mortal remains? And do the adjectives *mortal* and *immortal* even apply? What about his emotional remains, his spiritual remains? Let's get everything out here and in the box, please, before we close that lid. Don't want to leave anything behind in the funeral home, do we?

And how about that moniker, funeral home? What was homey about it? A home is a place where one lives daily, and I don't think any funeral passing through ever left a body for residence unless those immortal remains were stacked in the back somewhere. Why not a funeral lodge, or funeral gatehouse, since the mortician was, if anything, a gatekeeper?

We were riding that morning in two cars. Joel was driving his, with him Rita and two cousins who'd be pallbearers. Rachel and I were in the backseat of Uncle Harry and Aunt Bev's car, Harry driving. I started telling Rachel how silly it was to call a mortuary a funeral home: no home there, and the funeral happened elsewhere.

"It really doesn't matter, Karl," she said.

She took both my hands, held them in hers, smiled at me indulgently.

Rachel was an incredibly lovely woman. A light brunette, she had long eyebrows, long lashes, high chiseled cheekbones, wide full lips. The few light crow's feet at the corners of her eyes were pleasantly crinkled, as if shaped by smiling, and she did smile often, as she was now. She was gentle, soft-spoken, amiable. Her eyes were pale blue with a hint of green, a gift from some forgotten Viking ancestor. Living in Hawai'i, she swam and played tennis, kept herself in great shape. Any man she wanted would be putty in her hands. Little wonder she'd hooked an anesthesiologist. She could have had a pharmaceutical CEO had she aimed for one.

"Why call it a home, Rachel? It's such a misnomer."

"It's not important. There are so many little things that don't really matter, small things that don't make a difference. You'll be all right, Karl. Everyone will still call it a funeral home, but you'll be all right. I believe in you, Karl," she said.

I didn't know quite how to assimilate that. I liked being believed in. I felt elevated by her saying so: it felt good. A lot of people around Offenburg had told me they believed in Jesus Christ, and I started wondering if I weren't feeling at that moment the way Jesus felt all the time. Having people believe in him: I'm sure it perked Him up, even on a bad day.

"You have to come visit us, Karl. This spring, as soon as you get back," Rachel said.

"I will," I promised. "I'll schedule it first thing."

"You can't just schedule it, you have to do it. You schedule a lot of things you never do, Karl."

"I'll come; I promise. I love Hawai'i."

"I've always wanted to go there," Aunt Bev said. "They tell me you have a beautiful home, Rachel."

"We do, Aunt Bev. We're right by the water; we can walk to the beach. It'd be so wonderful to have you come."

"Do you hear that, Harry? We're invited. We should go."

"You know we can't just pick up and leave the farm," Uncle Harry said. "We have stock to care for."

"I know *you* can't pick up and leave," Aunt Bev said. "Other farmers manage to do it. Other farmers seem to be able to go on vacations."

"You have Joel," Rachel said. "He can take care of everything."

"Oh, I couldn't very well ask Joel to take care of everything so we could run off to Hawai'i. I wouldn't want to do that."

"Why not, Uncle Harry? I'm sure he'd be happy to. He'd love your coming to Hawai'i."

"I'm not so sure of that," Uncle Harry said.

"I'll ask him," Rachel said. "And you make Uncle Harry come, Aunt Bev. Have Joel take care of everything, and you make him come."

This was an interesting concept. Rachel knew as well as I that Aunt Bev in their nearly thirty-five years of marriage had never made Uncle Harry do anything. I'm sure Rachel could have made him, but Aunt Bev was a tune played on a different fiddle. It was likely she was never going to see Hawai'i. Not this marriage.

Finishing up at the funeral lodge was quick. Only we and the cousins who were pallbearers, the uncles and aunts who were their dads and moms, and ten or twelve neighbors—including Chris and Clara Kohler; Chris's dad and mom, August and Ada—were there. Nearly everyone stepped in front of the open coffin, stared for a moment at Dad, made the sign of the cross, and moved along. Rachel and I stood looking at him a long time. His face would go in and out of focus, and sometimes he was alive and stared back at me, and I could hear him asking if I was really going to stay in California forever, or if I was really not going to church anymore. Then I'd blink, and he'd be dead again, his flesh pasty and gray against the taffeta coffin lining, then alive again, even laughing as when I told him a story of a opossum biting a basketball player when the guy tried to tie it to a basketball hoop, and I heard him cry out, "Some of the stories you tell, Karl. Where do you get them?" Then dead again, eyelids shut, forehead permanently wrinkled. Still, unsmiling.

"It's not good to see him like this the last time," I said.

Rachel nodded, kissed her fingertips, and planted a kiss lightly on Dad's closed lips.

"Goodbye, Daddy," she said, barely audible.

It seemed the right thing to do. I kissed my fingertips, planted a kiss on his closed lips too, and told him, "Goodbye, Dad."

When Rachel and I moved aside, Joel and Rita took our places by the casket. It seemed we'd paired off like that inadvertently: Rita and Joel, the oldest and youngest; Rachel and me, the middle children, if you counted Rachel, born those seven minutes after Rita, as a middle child.

Rachel was holding my arm. Joel and Rita were not touching each other. It occurred to me Rachel might have been assigned to shadow me, that perhaps Rita had singled me out as the sibling most likely to crack at the funeral, the child most likely to behave rudely by Offenburg standards. Maybe Uncle Harry had ratted me out. Anything was possible. You bury your dad only once, and I'm sure Rita had a concept of how she wanted it done. No one loves insubordination more than I, but I'd show her. I could funeral with Rita or anyone.

After all mourners passed by the coffin and said their goodbyes, there was more praying, albeit brief, and the mortician closed the lid. Pallbearers rolled the coffin through the room and lifted it into the hearse parked outside. Everyone piled into a car, and across town to St. Barnabas we went, hearse leading, car with four pallbearers immediately behind. When we got to the church, everyone, including the drivers, got out of the cars. Attendants were waiting to park them.

The pallbearers pulled the coffin out and set it on a church truck. Into the church and up the main aisle they pushed it. The small choir broke into their version of "Ave Maria."

"Ave Dominus tecum, Benedicta tu in mulieribus. Et benedictus, Benedictus fructos ventris tui."

"Blessed is the fruit of thy womb" seemed a preposterous metaphor. It stuck in my craw, and I couldn't help but think of fruit—pears, apples, figs—and wonder if Dad had been low hanging fruit Jesus grabbed as he was passing through one evening. I could see Dad dropping from that rafter, rope quivering taut, but no Jesus standing there to catch him. Just the cold and dark woodshed and Dad's body twitching and the block of wood he'd stood on rolling slowly across the woodshed floor at about the pace the coffin was rolling up the church aisle. It seemed to take forever, but I didn't scream.

"O mater, puerum suum supplicem audire!"

When the coffin stopped and everyone had settled in pews, Father Rieschel came out and prayed over the box, sprinkled some holy water on it, waved a censer over it, pivoted, and shook the censer toward the altar for reasons probably known only to himself. Which was fine, because it got him headed in the right direction. He was quickly to the altar and into the Mass and got us through it in a half hour, would have got us through it faster if half the congregation hadn't shuffled up to the altar to receive communion. The pew behind us emptied. Joel got up and moved forward; Rita stayed seated. The pew in front of us started to go. Rachel poked Rita. "Come on," she whispered. Rita shook her head no. Rachel stepped past her and I followed, into the parade to receive the body of Christ. If Rachel could do it, I could. I knew she didn't go to church anymore, but she didn't seem to care. I hadn't been to confession in years and knew I was unworthy to receive the Eucharist, but I knelt with Rachel anyway. The priest placed a wafer on her tongue, then on mine, and I wondered crazily if Dad might be watching, if all along he'd really had it right and was with us. I couldn't for the life of me decide, if he were watching, whether he'd be pleased or horrified. The moment passed, and I knew it was pointless. I followed Rachel back to our pew. Rita moved her legs to let us pass, shaking her head as we slipped by.

The graveyard was close to the church so we walked. Pallbearers slid the coffin inside the hearse, and we lined up behind it: Father Rieschel and his servers, Joel and Rita, Rachel and me, Uncle Harry and Aunt Bev. Other relatives, neighbors, and friends came after us, pouring down the church steps and lining up in pairs to follow the slow-moving hearse along the pavement the few hundred yards to the cemetery. Inside the gates, the road was graveled. Tires crunched as they rolled toward the open grave. The morning was bitter cold, ground frozen, sun bright. Patches of frost still glistened around the edges of the mat thrown over the dirt at the graveside. Pallbearers backed the coffin out, carried it across the grass, and placed it on the straps that would lower it into the open earth. The crowd gathered, and Father Rieschel began his Rite of Committal.

"In your mercy look upon this grave, so that your servant Ernest Schroeder may sleep here in peace; and on the day of judgment raise him up to dwell with your saints in Paradise. We ask this through Christ our Lord."

A direct contract, God and Ernie Schroeder, with Jesus as realtor. What could go wrong? And it was only a holding plot, a place to rot until the day of judgment, assuming Christ heard. After all, we were just asking; there was no certainty. Viewing it that way, I felt better, though the cold earth bothered me. While Father Rieschel intoned, I kept thinking how deep the frost would penetrate when the coffin was lowered and covered. The body would be six feet under. Even on the coldest day in January, which surely this one damn near was, the ground would freeze less than a foot down. The frost would never touch him, and I whispered that to him. I thought it more important he know the frost wouldn't get to him than hear this being-raised-up-day-of-judgment gibberish.

"May his soul and the souls of all the faithful, departed through the mercy of God, rest in peace," Father Rieschel prayed.

"Amen," we answered.

I couldn't imagine Dad's soul, whatever a soul might be, at peace. I couldn't imagine anything about him ever at peace. His was not a desperate depression but an enfeebling anxiety. He worried about everything, was anxious about everything. The grief he knew at his wife's death wasn't enough; he worried about the salvation of her immortal soul too. Those first weeks after Mom died, we'd find him in unlikely places around the farm, kneeling and praying. In the barn hall one evening after having finished milking, he'd set the full bucket of milk in the straw and knelt to pray. When I asked if something had happened, he said, "No, your mother just asked me to pray for her." There wasn't anything crazy about that—she could have asked him in the weeks before she died—but that wasn't what he meant. He meant he'd just heard her ask and had dropped to his knees to pray. Which was different. No way she could ask him anything. She was dead.

This went on for months. After Mom died, Joel and I slept together in the same room as Dad. The girls shared a bedroom upstairs. One night I woke up because he was praying aloud. I turned on the light by our bed. He was kneeling at the foot of his, the cross of his rosary in his left hand, rapidly fingering the beads with his right. The cross was cutting into his palm, blood oozing down his wrist.

"Please turn out the light, Karl," he said.

"Your hand is bleeding, Dad."

He opened his hand and looked at it thoughtfully. The small metal crucifix was embedded in his skin like an arrowhead. It toppled into his palm as we gazed at it. He closed his hand on the blood, picked up the rosary, laid it on the bedspread, then said to me, "Turn off the light, Karl. Go to sleep now."

I turned off the light.

In the darkness I heard him go to the kitchen, I assumed to wrap the hand. I was still awake when he came back. He didn't get into bed right away. He knelt again, presumably to finish his rosary, but I couldn't be sure. He didn't pray aloud, and I fell asleep.

In spite of all the prayer over all the years, God ignored him big time. The wife died, he was sent away to a mental institution, his brother-in-law had to pay the note to save his farm, his son went off to college and abandoned his faith, his daughters moved away. I think he truly believed in a god who knew and saw his suffering, a god who'd reward him if he could bear it, but that god remained unresponsive. So maybe he believed out of desperation, perhaps understood he could not handle his life alone and then turned to God, instead of other people, for help. Maybe it dawned on Dad his last night that God was not a player, not even on the roster: he could call the game himself. He wasn't angry at the years of wasted tribulation and prayer; he knew finally he could be free. He could end the pain and anguish and loneliness himself, and he did. It was not a matter of his soul resting in peace; it was a matter of stopping a life of torment.

Aunt Bev said we needed to get going. The ladies of the parish sodality had prepared an after-funeral lunch. We were the main guests. She urged us to hurry, so we did, tramping *en masse* across the frozen winter grass, down the graveled cemetery road, out through the gates. As we passed the church, we could hear the tractor loader fire up to shovel back into the grave the dirt it had dug out. It wouldn't take long—a loader dump or two—until the coffin would be covered, the grave closed.

VIII

I drove Dad's Chevy back to California. Joel didn't need it, Rachel wasn't taking it to Hawai'i, Rita didn't want it. It was a fine car, so I took it.

Before I headed west, I swung through Chicago to say goodbye to Rita. Because it was biting cold, we spent most of our time in her apartment on West Roscoe Street, but one afternoon went downtown, hiked along the Lakefront Trail and out onto the Navy Pier. The pier had not been renovated; we passed boarded-up windows and chain link fences, then stopped along the south side, out of the wind. The beam from the lighthouse out on the lake flashed through the gray afternoon. The lake was rough outside the breakwater, a line of whitecaps charging south. The water near us was calm and dark blue, protected by the pier.

"You have to come back in the summer," Rita said. "It's much nicer then."

"I promised Rachel I'd come to Hawai'i. Maybe we could all meet there," I said.

"That would be fine," Rita said. "I'll check with Rachel to set it up. We have to stay together, you know. We have to stay in touch."

I watched her warily, wondering what she was getting at. She had turned from me and was looking out toward the lighthouse. Her cheeks and nose were rosy from the cold.

"You know we always knew it would end this way. We grew up expecting it to end this way," she said.

"Not me. I never really expected this."

"Are you dense, Karl? He'd tried before. You knew that. How could you forget the night we found him in the barn? What do you think he was doing out there?"

Rita woke me in the middle of the night, told me to get up, to come with her, that Dad had gone out of the house but hadn't come back. She had on her coat, held a flashlight. She told Rachel to get in bed with Joel, who didn't even wake up. I don't know why she wanted me, instead of Rachel, to go with her.

"I've always wondered why you wanted me, and not Rachel, to go with you to the barn that night."

"I don't know, Karl," she said.

We found Dad sitting on a feed bucket in the corn crib. He too had a flashlight, which he'd set on the floor. His twelve-gauge pump action shotgun was lying in his lap. He was leaning over it, arms across the stock and barrel. He seemed distracted and didn't hear us come in.

"Dad," Rita said, "was there something out here? A coyote? A raccoon?"

"Yes, there was something. I don't know what it was."

"But you heard something?"

"No, I didn't hear anything. I know something was out here, though, and I just sat down to think about it."

"Whatever it was is gone," Rita said. "Come back in the house with us now."

He got up, picked up his flashlight and shotgun, walked with us back to the house. Rita quickly led the way, shining her light in front, me in the middle, Dad following. We went in through the kitchen door. Rita turned on a light and told Dad to put the gun back on the rack above the cabinet, and he did.

"Let's go to bed," Rita said, and we went into the bedroom where Rachel was covered up to her chin with blankets. Joel was still asleep. Dad sat on his bed.

"You aren't going to sleep in your clothes, are you?" Rita asked.

"No," Dad said.

"Then take off your shoes."

She stood in the middle of the room watching Dad while he took off his shoes and socks. Then she turned and said, "Come, Rachel. I have to pee."

"I remember coming back from the barn," I said. "You were in front, going very fast. You seemed to know exactly what you were doing."

"I was never more scared in my life," Rita said.

"I was never scared of Dad."

"You should have been. A lunatic dad with a loaded shotgun walked behind us that night."

"And you knew that then?"

"I knew I had to get help," she said.

"Come on, Dad," she said that night, "get your clothes off, go to bed. You don't have to wait up for us."

Kicking his shoes partially under the bed as she went past, Rita hurried out of the bedroom with Rachel, through the kitchen to the backyard, to our outhouse. Dad sat on his bed but didn't take off his coveralls. I took off my jeans and crawled in.

"Aren't you getting in bed?" I asked.

"I can wait 'til they get back. I wouldn't want to lie down until they're back in the house."

"It takes them a long time; it always takes them a long time. I'm going to sleep."

I turned on my belly but didn't sleep. I watched Dad out of one eye. He didn't seem tired or anxious about the girls. He sat very still, hands in lap, and stared into the room. After a while he shifted and looked under the bed for his shoes.

"I wonder what's taking them so long," he said.

"Maybe they fell in."

"Don't say things like that, Karl."

"They're not going to fall in, Dad."

He shifted again and waited again, reached under the bed for his socks and shoes again.

"I better go see what's keeping them."

"They'll be back, Dad. They both probably had to pee."

It was taking them a long time, and Dad knew it.

"I'm going to check," he said.

He started putting on his socks, not hastily as if he were panicked, just pulling on each one slowly before he reached for a shoe. He'd put on one shoe, and tied it, and was reaching for the second when a car pulled into the driveway and footsteps came running to the kitchen door. Dad hobbled toward the disturbance, trying to pull the second shoe on and walk at the same time. I jumped out of bed, following him out of the bedroom and into the kitchen. Rita and Rachel rushed in to hug Dad as Uncle Harry reached up to the gun rack and took down the shotgun. He pumped it three times fast; three shells snicked out, skidding across the linoleum, one flying across the stovetop with a loud ping. Aunt Bev was standing in the doorway.

"What are you doing, Harry?" Dad asked, leaning toward him but not moving. Rita and Rachel were clinging to him. He had his arms around them too as if he didn't want to let go.

Uncle Harry didn't answer. He took the shotgun outside, tossed it in the trunk of his car, locked it, and came back quickly. He was standing in the doorway beside Aunt Bev when Joel came waddling in, sleepy-eyed and frightened. Joel started to wail and climbed into Dad's arms, past Rita and Rachel. Dad sat on a chair so he could hold all of them.

"If you'd taken me with you to the outhouse, I could have run with you to Uncle Harry's faster than Rachel."

"Karl, that's funny. I never went alone to the outhouse at night, but I never took you, ever. I always took Rachel. You knew that, Dad knew that."

"It amazes me you ran all the way to Uncle Harry's in the time we waited for you to pee."

"It's less than a half mile, and it was dark."

"It was still very fast."

"Thirteen-year-olds run fast in the dark, especially when they're scared," she said.

"You were only a kid, Rita. I forget that."

"Yes, I was only a kid," Rita said. "I don't forget."

IX

Four years after the funeral, I went back for Joel's wedding. I arrived early and spent a week with my brother before the crowd began to gather. He'd renovated the old farmhouse. The screened porch was gone, replaced with a utility-washroom and office. The front porch had been extended the full length of the house, and we spent our evenings sitting there, sipping beer, talking far into the night. A lot of cousins and friends came by. There was ribaldry about marriage and razzing of Joel about losing his freedom. He bore it well, I thought. I realized he didn't mind being the center of attention, which surprised me.

I rode around the farm with him, in his pickup or on his tractor, to replace rotten fenceposts in a hillside pasture fence, or drop salt blocks—the things a farmer does to keep his spread in order. Although he was getting married Saturday, he was still mindful of his chores. Wednesday, we reinforced the lot fence below the barn, adding two-by-four top railings where planks had broken. Thursday morning we gathered his cattle, all sixty-four brood cows and their calves, herding them into a holding pen behind the corral. The calves had some kind of flu and diarrhea, and each cow and calf had to get an antibiotic injection. The lot was configured with a series of gates to crowd cattle toward a squeeze chute designed for catching an animal and holding it safely. Joel laid out his antibiotics, syringes, and needles on a shelf above the chute, adjusted it for the cows, checked the back trap and front release, then announced he was ready.

We drove the herd into the corral using gates to pen them closer, crowding them until they were packed tight against the chute, then shooed a cow in. Joel closed the rump bar, jabbed the full syringe in her shoulder with his right hand, and tripped the headgate release lever to set her free with his left. One by one we ran each cow through. Wearing heavy coveralls and knee-high rubber boots, I slipped into the pen to drive the last ones in. After all the cows had shots, Joel adjusted the chute for calves, and we started them through. Most were winter calves, probably weighing less than two hundred pounds, but they were stubbornly hard to get into the chute. I used gates to shrink the lot as the number of untreated calves dwindled. Within time we were down to a dozen, then six, then two. When one of the two entered the chute and Joel closed the trap on it, the remaining calf realized it was alone in the pen. It had no intentions of staying and leapt against the wooden fence, trying to scramble over it.

"Catch that bastard!" Joel shouted. "We can't let one get away. They all have to get shots."

He jabbed the syringe into the second-to-last calf and tripped the chute to free it. I grabbed the hind legs of the calf trying to climb out and pulled him off the fence.

"Hold that son-of-a-bitch!" Joel yelled, charging toward us with his syringe.

I held that son-of-a-bitch, though he pulled me off my feet and dragged me around the corral. Joel chased us until he popped the needle into the calf's shoulder.

"Done! Let him go."

I didn't have to be told twice. My torso had plowed along the ground like a bulldozer. My chest was resting on a mound of shit, my face and hair spattered with bits of wet calf ooze.

Laughing, Joel sat down in the cow shit next to me. The last calf kept running in a circle around us.

"I wish you could see yourself," Joel said. "Don't lick your lips right now."

"It's only cow shit."

"It's hard to believe you'll ever be clean enough to fit a tuxedo."

"Maybe I can wear this and add new meaning to being a shitty pick for best man."

"I don't think so. It's going to be hard enough for me to look at you in a tux and not laugh my ass off thinking of you covered in shit."

"I'll do everything I can to remind you. When the preacher asks for anyone to speak now or forever hold his peace, I might bring this up."

"We cut that from the ceremony. You'll never get a chance to say anything," Joel said. "This shit's between you and me."

After I'd taken a shower, we headed to Jefferson City to be fitted for those tuxedos. Joel chuckled from time to time as he drove. I didn't need to ask what amused him. Sprawled in the corral with six inches of shit under my chest, I'd been worth a laugh. Cleaned up, even I found it amusing. And Joel was far from keeping this shit between us. He told the story to the young women in the formal wear and bridal shop where we picked up the tuxedos; he'd tell it at his bachelor's party; he'd tell it at the rehearsal dinner. The only time he didn't tell it was at the wedding.

On our way back from Jefferson City, we swung through Offenburg to pick up kegs for the bachelor party. His buddies were buying, Joel picking up. He drove through town along Main Street, passed the liquor outlet without stopping, and pulled into the parking lot at St. Barnabas.

"You got something we need to pray about?" I asked.

"I want you to see Dad's headstone. You haven't yet."

"I don't want to see no tombstone."

"Why not?"

I tried to think of why I didn't but really had no reason. I didn't want to walk through a cemetery. I didn't want to look at a tombstone.

"I don't know. I just know I don't want to."

"Aw come on, Karl. It won't hurt you."

"I'm here for your wedding, Joel. I'm here to celebrate. I'm not here to go see some goddamn tombstone."

"Come on. We can celebrate that we're here together to visit Dad's grave. I haven't been by here myself in a while."

He got out of the pickup. I got out. The sound of the truck doors slamming echoed off the church wall. We strolled along the pavement past the church and toward the cemetery. The rectory sign still hung above the parsonage. It was completely still and, in the bright afternoon sunlight, cast a perfect rectangular shadow. I thought about Joel not having been by here himself in a while.

"You come to visit his grave often?" I asked.

"Not often."

"Once a week, once a month?"

"When I'm around, I come by. Since I'm with Ellie, I'm not over here much."

We passed through the cemetery gates, which were open, followed the winding graveled road through the graveyard, and cut across between tombstones to the plot where Dad was buried. The grass was recently mown. Our footsteps stirred up a fresh-cut fragrance.

The headstone was a simple gray, square slab about three feet high, curved slightly across the top. A white cross the size of a hand was chiseled into the upper center of the stone. Dad's name was centered below it, followed by his dates of birth and death: ERNEST ALFRED SCHROEDER, 1926–1984. Below that the universal message: REST IN PEACE.

"Do you talk to him when you come here?" I asked.

"Sometimes."

"He's not here, you know. You could just as well talk to him on the farm."

"His bones are down there. Aren't none of his bones on the farm."

"What do you tell him?"

"Come on, Karl. Sometimes I tell him what a brain-dead brother I have, but I usually have better things to talk about."

I let that go. Probably deserved it. Joel leaned forward and flicked bits of cut grass off the granite base of the stone, then crossed to the next grave, our mother's, and cleaned the grass off her marker too. Hers too was a simple stone, marked with a cross and her name: BERNICE CALLAHAN SCHROEDER, 1924–1963, REST IN PEACE.

"I couldn't quite match the color," Joel said.

"Looks close to me."

"Close, but not a match. They can't get that stone anymore."

"Do you talk to her too, Joel?"

"No."

"Do you remember her?"

"No."

"You were four the year she died."

"That's what they tell me. Do you remember her?"

"A little, but not much."

"Did you get mad at her too for dying, the way you did with Dad?"

"No. She didn't kill herself."

"You still mad at Dad?"
"Some, but not so much."
"That's good."
"What's good about it? Maybe I should still be on his case."
"Everybody has to let go, Karl. Even you can't keep it up forever."
"You okay with it, Joel?"
"I live with it. When I come here, it seems to me even if he'd not died the way he did, what he'd have wanted most would be to lie here next to our mom. He would have wanted it that way, and he has it."
"He doesn't know it."
"Doesn't matter. It would have been what he wanted."
"I don't get this being buried side by side. Beloved Parents of Leo and JoAnn. Beloved Wife and Husband. Sometimes one headstone over both graves. If they want to be together dead, why not drop 'em in the same coffin? Pop the lid, toss the second in with the first, body on the bones of the beloved. Much closer than two graves."
"You certainly have some crazy ideas, Karl."
"If I ever marry, I think I'll have her stuffed in the same box with me. I'll want her where my bones can hold her."
"You better get that in the prenuptial," Joel said.
"Do you?"
"Don't need it. I'm like Dad. I'll be satisfied planted next to Ellie," Joel said.

We walked back, not talking, down the graveled cemetery road, out through the cemetery gates, and climbed into the pickup before either of us said anything.
"How's Dad's old car doing?" Joel asked. That didn't surprise me. I too thought of it as Dad's old car.
"The car's fine," I said.

X

I still have that car. You can't wear out a Chevy. I don't know why Dad always traded for a newer model. An old work jacket of Dad's was in the car when I got to California; I've kept it in the trunk. Years before, I'd tossed the piece of rope from the woodshed in the trunk and kept it until a hiking trip with a woman I'd met only eight weeks before. Right away we saw each other every day, dined together most nights, breakfasted together most mornings. She said she loved backpacking, a favorite pastime of mine. As soon as we were free for a few days, we headed for the Trinity Alps.

We drove Dad's old car. When we were pulling packs out of the trunk at the trailhead, the rope came out. I picked it up and put it back.

"What's that?" she asked.

On a hiking trip, you don't want to scare someone before you've even started, but you don't want to lie either.

"The rope my dad hanged himself with," I said. "He committed suicide."

"And you take it with you backpacking?"

"No. I just keep it in the trunk."

"Bring it. It doesn't look heavy."

I put it in an outside pocket of my backpack.

"When?" she asked.

"Eight years ago."

"I see," she said.

I had no idea what she saw.

We hiked hard that day, up the Stuart Fork of the Trinity, fourteen miles to Emerald Lake below Sawtooth Mountain, through country as gorgeous as you'd find anywhere: acres of wildflowers, tons of waterfalls, soaring walls of granite. We didn't talk much, but from time to time she'd ask me something about my dad, and I'd tell her about his struggles and how he'd killed himself and how sometimes, but not often, I was still pissed at him for having done it. By the time we made camp and were sitting by a small fire off from the lake, she'd heard about everything there was to tell. Like most campers tuckered out the first day, we were pretty quiet, sipping a bit of brandy we'd carried in. When we did talk, she went back to my being miffed at Dad's suicide.

"Get the rope. Your pack's right there," she said.

I took the rope out.

"Throw it in the fire," she said. "Get rid of it."

I wasn't sure, but she was. I threw it on the fire. The polyester cord melted, burned brightly, and was gone.

"Now take out your anger," she said, holding her hands, palms open, toward me. "I'll get rid of it for you."

"Are you kidding?"

"Just give me your anger. I'll get rid of it."

"That's preposterous."

"No more preposterous than being pissed eight years at your dad for killing himself. Get it out."

She shook her hands impatiently in a *give-me* gesture. I mimicked pulling anger out of my head and cupping my hands to give it to her.

"Not out of your head, Karl," she scolded. "Out of your heart, out of your core."

I repeated the mimicry of pulling out anger, out of my chest this time, and again mimicked handing it to her. She got up and disappeared into the darkness. She was wearing a headlamp but didn't turn it on, and I couldn't follow where she was going or what she was doing. Was she flinging the anger everywhere, scattering it like ashes? Was she taking it apart bit by bit and tossing it away? Was she hunting old mining equipment abandoned around the lake where she could hide the anger so I couldn't find it the next morning? I didn't know. I sat by the fire, stared at a sky full of stars, talked to Dad.

"You're screwing with me tonight again," I said. "My woman's out there roaming the dark, scattering my anger when there's nothing in the world I want more than to get her in the tent. I'm not going to carry you around anymore, Dad. You're on your own. Get used to it."

She wasn't gone long. When she came back, she stood facing the fire, hands in her back pants pockets.

"Well, that's done," she said. "You ready for the tent?"

"Sure," I said.

I may be a fool, but I'm not foolish. I married that woman. Not that I believed for a moment she'd taken my anger and dumped it in the Trinity Alps. But she was right about one thing: it was time to let it go, and I did.

Two years later, our daughter was born. The morning I walked in to bring mother and child home, she was nestled in her mother's arms, head braced against a pillow, staring straight out at the world. There was no expression on her face. She couldn't smile yet, and I didn't know if she could even see me, but her eyes didn't wander. She stared with the same blank expression my dad had so often thrown at me—not of condemnation, not of amusement, but simple incomprehension of a world, or a son, too bizarre to decipher.

At that moment, I wished so much he were still alive, that he could meet our child, could stand beside me watching her, could share with me that stare of incomprehension on his granddaughter's face, but it wasn't going to happen. It was something to regret, and I regretted it terribly, but it was nothing to be angry about. Not anymore.

Friends

The phone rang. I was in the house midmorning, when I would normally have been outside. I spent a lot of that summer on a scaffold scratching paint off gutters, eaves, and window frames. Prepping the house for painting, I had scraped and scoured most of the overhanging wood of the upper story. On a two-storied Victorian, no small accomplishment. I took the call; it was Elia.

"Can you come over?" she asked.

"What's happening?"

"Connor needs you?"

"For what?"

"I can't explain; he needs you. Can you come?"

"If he really needs me."

"He really does," she said. "Please come."

I lowered the two ladders I'd been using. There was no leaving them propped against the house in a neighborhood full of children who loved to climb. Gathering my tools, I stored them in the garage, backed the car out, and took the closest ramp east on Interstate 80.

Connor and Elia lived in Carmichael, a suburb of Sacramento, where they owned and operated a private pre- and K-4 primary school dedicated to art for youth. Connor joked the school was rich on youth, lean on art, gaunt on cash. They offered scholarships to any child who applied but didn't have the wherewithal for private school—not a good model for business but an admirable practice for a school.

They were a wonderfully urbane couple. Both had been actors, dancers; both were handsome—he Irish, ruddy, gray-haired; she Jewish, charismatic, poised. They glided into a room, any room, as if the script called for their entrance and other players should be prepared to acknowledge them.

"Has the band showed up yet?" Connor liked to shout, his intimation that he'd come to party and, when they entered a room, the celebrating always ratcheted up. Laughter got louder, drinks flowed more freely. Sacramento was a drinking town, as most political towns are.

We came to know Connor and Elia when my wife, Anna, decided our daughter would benefit from a more rigorous preschool than the daycare she attended. Visiting the school in Carmichael, Anna was as taken with Elia as she was with the curriculum. When Elia talked about kinesthetic learning and leapt up to demonstrate with a chasse or perfect flat-back, Anna was mesmerized. She enrolled Chloe.

I was drawn to Connor as a father figure and friend. At the time we met, I was a consulting civil engineer, working only when I had a project. Projects had been few and far between. We'd just bought the Victorian for what I thought an obscene price; I was scared shitless how we'd pay for it. Connor became the confidant who allayed my fear.

"Don't worry about debt," he said. "It's like a bruise. It's ugly at first, but goes away. Monthly payments, interest, taxes become routine."

"What if we don't have the money? What if we can't get it?"

"The money's always out there. You're educated, you're bright. You'll get your share."

"But if we don't, we're in deep shit."

"It doesn't work that way. Wounds always heal," Connor said. "It's the way of the world."

He was an eternal optimist, a "one-door-closes, three-open" kind of guy. In his late fifties, he had almost twenty years on me, liked to assure me that any problem had a solution, any catastrophe an ending. He didn't always know or have the solution or ending, but he believed it was out there.

"Bad things happen to good people," I argued.

“Indeed they do, but even bad things tend to work out. It’s not circumstances that crumple people; it’s how you live or can’t live with them.”

He believed anyone who really wanted to succeed would succeed. “The arc of living bends toward success,” he liked to say, and his life was testimony to it. Unable to support his family as an actor, he became a salesman. “One of the best,” he said, which I didn’t doubt, but it bored him. He liked crowds and children and loved Elia. She’d always wanted a school where learning was focused on dance. As soon as their children were out of the house, they sold it and bought the property they would transform into Elia’s dream. Connor cut his hours as a salesman and focused on building the school.

He was still adding rooms, realigning storage areas, building play structures, and landscaping when Chloe started there. Days I drove her, I often stayed to help him. He was a more skilled carpenter than I—had those twenty years on me—and I was always looking to learn something. And he was a joy to work with.

One of the first things he said was, “I don’t know what carpenters you’ve worked with, but here we never miss anything by a cunt hair. We never bang a stud a C hair to the right, we never trim a board a C hair shorter. I don’t like that expression.”

As the father of a child I was sure would grow up to be a feminist, I was fine with that.

“What do we use? Off by a boar bristle, off by a ‘bb’?”

“Silly millimeter. We’re in a school yard. Silly millimeter seems right.”

We built a silly millimeter sculpture, the base a teepee of four pieces of wood cut too short. When we cut a piece we couldn’t use, which didn’t happen often, we tacked it to the silly millimeter sculpture. Decent carpenters find ways to use even the shortest miscuts; expert carpenters do not miscut. Connor and I were somewhere between the two. After a few months, the structure became a short misshapen totem pole we set out when we started a job and took back in when we finished. The kids were free to paint it anytime they chose, as many times as they chose. They loved it. In time it became as varicolored as misshapen. Since gathering tools and cleanup was my specialty, I was the totem pole keeper and brought it in any afternoon I was helping with the pergola, steps, fence or whatever we'd worked on that day. I would check with Connor if I was free to go.

"You're finished," he'd say. "Drive safely."

"I will," I'd assure him.

"Keep it in your knickers," he'd add.

"You too," I'd shoot back.

That he'd not use a term such as "C hair" in carpentry but caution "keep it in your knickers" as valediction was no contradiction. For Connor respect for women was a necessary part of enlightenment—ribaldry among men testimony to their not having fully attained it.

Conrad and Elia lived adjacent to the school in a sprawling ranch-style home modified with additional windows, skylights, interior halls, and walls for hanging art. Their collection was extensive and eclectic, mostly from artists they'd known in Los Angeles or Sacramento before their work had been recognized: Thiebaud, Ruscha, Robert Dowd.

I parked in the driveway and crossed the school yard to their house.

Elia let me in. She hugged me, smiled as always, but looked as if she'd been touring a battlefield.

"What's happened?" I asked.

"Connor's in the living room," she said, pointing me down the hall.

He was sitting in an armchair usually reserved for reading, his shoulders slumped, hands in lap, head bowed. He looked up when I walked in and stared at me, shaking his head from side to side.

"What's going on, Connor?"

"I killed a man," he said.

"What are you saying?"

"I killed a man. That's what I'm saying."

"That makes no sense, Connor. Then why are you here?"

"Yes, it makes no sense. Indeed it makes no sense, but it happened. I hit someone in a crosswalk."

"Where?"

"Does it matter where? I hit him and killed him. Over on Winding Way, toward Manzanita, not far from here. We know the family—the Harbergers, Ronan and Kerry."

I stared at him, then at the floor, searching for words, not something that would offer solace but that would allow us to talk about what happened. My standing appeared to irritate him.

"Please sit down," he said.

I sat but still came up with few words or gestures. I did think of standing and shouting, "Stop it! Cut the theatrics!" convincing myself for a second these two old actors were working their way through a scene in a dismal play, trying a dry run out on me. It was damned effective. Let the scene end. Bring up the house lights, for God's sake. Tempting as I found it, the fancy didn't last. There were no house lights.

I almost asked if he'd been drinking, but thought better of it. Connor and Elia partied hard, and often, and Connor drove home buzzed often, I suspect, if not legally drunk. He'd picked up a DUI two years previous, for an alcohol level of 0.088. Barely over the top, he liked to point out, but it counted anyway. I thought of the crosswalk, thought of the Mrs. McGrath lyrics: *Now were ye drunk or were ye blind / When ye left yer two fine legs behind? With your too-ria, fol-diddle di-a.*

"Were you arrested?" I asked.

"Yes. I was hauled in."

"I wasn't drinking," he volunteered.

"I didn't ask."

"You might have been thinking it. Many will. We had a couple of beers after work—we'd closed that contract with the West Placer County school district—but I wasn't shit-faced, not even the 0.08 shit-faced they check for. I just hit him. I didn't see him, and I hit him."

"So why did they arrest you?"

"I killed him. I deserved to be arrested."

"You failed the field sobriety test?"

"I refused the test. My lawyer told me never to take the FST. The cops don't like that. Oh no they don't! So they arrested me. He was dead; his head was cracked on the pavement. There was blood across the yellow stripes in the crosswalk. They were right to arrest me."

How the accident had happened was less important to him than that it had happened. He wasn't clear about details. To him it seemed impossible he'd killed a man, as it seemed impossible to me. How could I absorb that? How could he?

Connor was on his way home from the cabinet shop where he worked those few hours a week, traveling east on Winding Way, driving the speed limit at approximately 30 mph, he said. Later, the accident reconstruction expert hired by the insurance company would estimate his speed at 35 to 40 mph. The street was four lanes wide, two in each direction, no divider. A van was stopped in the right lane, signaling a turn. Assuming the van was turning right, Connor swung around it. A pedestrian he hadn't seen was in the crosswalk. He slammed on the brakes but struck the pedestrian. The man was not run over, but he was lying on the street. First responders rushed him to a hospital. He was dead on arrival.

"It was Ronan Harberger's father-in-law, Paul Thoresson," Connor said. "He's older and had been staying with them. He was hard of hearing, probably didn't hear me coming. But he knew he was going to be hit. He looked at me just before I hit him. He hadn't time to be startled. He didn't look scared, just surprised. It gets me."

"I'm sure it does. I'm sorry, Connor."

"I'm sorry. Jesus, I'm sorry."

For most of the next hour we sat in silence. I could hear Connor breathing. Occasionally he'd moan; occasionally he'd say, "Oh shit." Just that, "Oh shit." A bird chirped in the foliage above the patio for a while, then was still. A car horn blew once. The room was quiet, but something horrific was in it. Not horrific just to Connor but inherently horrific. It hung from the walls, the ceiling. It covered the chairs, the mantle, the sideboard. It filled the room, and not speech, or thought, or hope could remove it. Nor was there compulsion to have it gone. It seemed necessary to allow it to be there, even to want it not to go away.

"Let's go for a ride," I said finally.

"I don't know," Connor said.

"Nothing says you have to hide in a dark room."

"Where would we go?"

"The river. Somewhere we like. Off Ice House Road, somewhere up there."

"Isn't that a little far?"

"What else you doing today? Might as well go where it's gorgeous as sit here."

Rivers were a retreat for almost everyone in Sacramento. Flowing along the west side, the Sacramento River separates the lived-in developed city to the east from farmland to the west in Yolo County. It's a large river pinched between levies, used by locals mainly for boating. The American, rushing down from the Sierra Nevada, divides the city north to south. Access to the American is easier than to the Sacramento; it's by far the more popular for swimming, kayaking, and picnicking. A favorite activity for our families was to leave the city, drive east on Highway 50 until it paralleled the South Fork of the American, or on Interstate 80 to where it paralleled the Middle Fork, and find a place to leave the highway and hike. Highway 50 and the South Fork was my plan.

I drove east and crossed the river on Sunrise Boulevard, planning our route to avoid the intersection where Connor had his accident.

"So, we're driving around where I did my killing?" he asked.

"I didn't think you'd want to go near it."

"Are you trying to spare me?"

"Did you want to?"

"No."

As we climbed away from Sacramento, from time to time Connor would turn and look back at the shrinking city as if checking for something, a pillar of salt perhaps, marking the spot of his accident, which he refused to call one.

"It wasn't an accident. I wasn't paying attention."

"Then what is an accident? You weren't paying attention, something happened. You didn't hit him deliberately."

"I killed him. I was in a hurry. I don't know why, and in a moment—no, much less than a moment—you can't snap your fingers fast enough to show how quickly it happened: I killed him."

"A split second?"

"Less than a split second. It wasn't, and then he was dead."

"That's why it's an accident."

"The world was different instantly when I wasn't expecting it. I changed it. I changed our world: mine, Elia's, Kevin's, Jodie's, Ronan and Kerry's, her father—the man I killed. I hurt everyone just like that, in less than a second."

"Yes, but you've always told me what happens is not as important as what you do with what happens."

"What can you do with killing a man?"

"What do you think? You get over it in time."

"I wish I'd been drunk, totally drunk, 0.8 on their goddamned scale. It'd make more sense. To kill him just by not paying attention makes no sense. It'd be better if I'd been drinking."

"Not so."

"Would he be less dead? Would it make any difference?"

"It'd make a hell of a difference. Anyone can hurt someone by not paying attention. It's an accident. Killing someone driving drunk is murder."

"That's a hell of a distinction."

"There is a difference between murder and manslaughter. You know that."

"The difference is horse pucky. The man is dead no matter which. I killed him."

"The man is dead, I killed him." This was the demon that had seized Connor's every thought, curled its fingers around his understanding as if it were a hand locked in rigor mortis. It seemed to fit him to think of the deed in that form, to hold it as close as possible, as if his only hope of not destroying himself was possessing it fully.

We didn't talk much as we drove through Cameron Park and Shingle Springs, then past Placerville. Above Pollock Pines, the highway climbed into forest. Lodgepole pines cast their shadows along the shoulder of the pavement. Past Pacific House, the road swung close to the river, and we could catch glimpses of white cascades below. We talked of stopping at the Bridal Veil Falls parking lot, but expected people there and wanted to be as much as possible by ourselves.

We pulled off the highway at Ice House Road. At least a dozen cars were parked east of the bridge, one pickup in the graveled turnout west of it. Parking in front of the pickup, we walked to the river, mostly in silence, and worked our way downstream to a gravel bar where we stopped.

Upstream, water poured through the canyon in a chute, hurling itself furiously toward where we stood, as if it would cut through the bar and slam into the canyon wall. The white water flattened, then slowed quickly, as if the river had frightened itself, had risked a flow that would have irrevocably changed its course. Rivers have that happen. At flood stage they pour down a slough and remain there, abandoning towns and locks and levees along their old channel. The unexpected happens. Same river, same water, never quite the same course.

"I loved my mother," Connor said. "I loved her more than I ever loved anyone. More than Elia, more than my children, Kev and Jodie, even."

"What's wrong with that?"

"I always fantasized I'd do anything to have her alive again. That's not true anymore. If Satan appeared suddenly before me in all his sulfurous stench offering me one wish for my soul, I'd choose that I'd never killed Paul Thoresson over having my mother alive."

"Understandable."

"I really loved my mother," Connor said.

We stood watching the water. After a while I left the sandbar and walked downstream along the bank. Connor followed. I stopped to wait for him at the first bend in the river.

"Satan would never come for my soul," Connor said when he caught up with me. "He already has it."

"Satan doesn't have your soul, Connor."

"I think a killer's soul belongs to Satan."

"You're not a killer."

"Then what am I?"

"A person who accidently took a life. That's not a killer."

"I killed that guy. I'm a killer. I'll always be."

"You'll rebuild yourself. You're not just someone who killed a pedestrian. You're a man with family and friends, a man who loves and cares for the people he loves. It's hard to see it now, but you will be whole."

"And how would that happen?"

"We're both old Catholic boys, right? Though neither of us has much faith anymore, there's value in what the Church teaches about forgiveness, especially forgiving the self when you've wronged someone grievously."

"Yes. I'd say I wronged him grievously."

"You're taking the first step: acknowledging that you've done wrong. The Church teaching is that you're heartily sorry you have sinned, totally, so that your heart will not be hardened against God or, in this case, hardened against yourself."

"You should have been a priest. I hate that platitudinous bullshit. It's why I left the Church."

"Throw out the holy water, but the Church gets some things right. There are steps, or stages, if you want to think of it that way, that every human needs to get through when he's done something terrible—especially if what he did, he did inadvertently."

"So what happens next?"

"You do a penance."

"What penance?"

"Anything. It's supposed to be voluntary. Think of something hard. Something physical. Wear a hair shirt for a month. Bodily mortification. The Church loves that. You could whack your pecker with a hammer once a day for a month."

"Jesus. I'm glad you're not my confessor."

"I'm not trying to be your confessor. I'm giving you some options."

"Whacking my pecker is not an option."

"Whatever. Penance is an act. You do something to expiate your wrong. After penance, you make restitution."

"Restitution?"

"Reparation for what's been done which you can't do fully, but you can try. You know the family. Find out what the dead father-in-law loved, and support it. Not necessarily money, but money too if they want it."

"I can't talk to them."

"You can't talk to them?"

"I want to. I want to tell them I'm sorry. I want to tell them how I wish the world could be set back a day and their father could be alive. I want to tell them how terribly, terribly I want that, but our lawyer says we can't even send a sympathy note. They're neighbors, people we know, but the lawyer says no contact. 'Absolutely no contact!' she says. 'If they contact you, you do not reply. It's critical,' she says."

"There are still ways to make restitution. For your sake. Find a charity they support. Give to it. You can do that without contacting them."

"Absolutely no contact, she says."

"So she says. She's your lawyer. But you have to take care of yourself. She's not going to."

We continued downstream for another half hour to where the current swept against the mountainside, blocking passage. We scrambled up the wall for a few hundred feet but stopped when the climb became treacherous. We rested, watched the river.

"She likes that word critical," Connor said. "It's critical that we not contact the Harbergers, it's critical that I not take an FST. Everything is critical."

I shrugged, but he wasn't really talking to me.

"It's critical that we not talk to news outlets; it's critical that we not talk at all; it's critical that our children not talk."

He started to laugh, an uncanny staccato cackle, closer to yowling than laughter. It echoed through the canyon.

"It's critical I cut my hair, critical I stay clean-shaven.

"'Wear shoes with laces,' she says. 'Wear matching socks. It's critical.'

"Oh, 'the thousand natural shocks that flesh is heir to.' Is not each of these too critical? I asked her.

"'It's not funny, Connor,' she said.

"But it is funny. It's too damned funny. It's not just CRITICAL. It's FUNNY!"

He roared critical and funny into the bright afternoon sunlight, which to him must have seemed a mockery of the dark self-loathing that possessed him.

"Critical!" he cried again, and again he laughed the unnerving yowl, and again bellowed "CRITICAL!"

"Stop it," I said.

"It won't stop."

"It will, Connor. It will in time."

He remained still for a long moment, absolutely still, staring past me. Doubting? Believing? I could not tell.

"Let's go," he said, standing up.

He followed me back to the car, a few steps behind, saying nothing.

On the return to Sacramento, late afternoon sun beating against the windshield, Connor fell asleep: for an hour at least, his horror at what he'd done was suspended. What he'd done, or what had happened to him? Which was it? He religiously referred to his having killed a man, and in his mind now, he knew he'd be defined forever by that violation, or at least marked by it. But what about his tenet, "wounds always heal"? "The way of the world," he'd said. Why should this wound remain an outlier? Time encrusts all things, layers living over memory; even the most regrettable act gets buried under everyday debris and reappears only in brief, unsettling moments—like the repaired crack in a countertop, noticed only when the kitchen is cleaned, the countertop scoured.

Connor would plead guilty to involuntary manslaughter without criminal negligence and serve no jail time. His lawyer ensured any sentence would be served in court-ordered community service.

For months after the accident, when I asked Connor how he was doing, he'd say, "I'm holding on."

And later he'd say, "Surviving. Struggling, but surviving."

Much later, he'd say, "I'm getting along. I'm getting there."

And one day he said, "Don't ask. It's not needed."

Wherever *there* in Connor's geography, it was not mine to pry. I stopped asking.

Evolution Valley

I

The boatman threw the line in a high arc toward the rock where the ferry had been moored. The outboard revved up; the boat backed away. It turned slowly, picking up speed as it headed into Florence Lake, trailing a wake that split the surface like a surgeon's knife, water opening like skin pulled back. The wound rubbed itself out as the V widened. A hundred yards behind the boat, the lake went smooth again.

"Healed quickly," Everett thought.

Other passengers gathered gear, climbed away from the landing. Everett dragged his backpack across the granite, sat down, and watched until the boat docked on the opposite shore and he could no longer hear the thrum of the motor. He picked up his walking stick, all wood, oak, biodegradable, including the leather wrist strap threaded through the top. Fifty-two inches long—he'd sized it when he bought it especially for this trip.

He placed the stick tip against the rock, hauled himself up with both hands, balancing carefully before he bent his knees and went down for his backpack. A frameless model he'd also bought especially for this trip, he'd packed it the night before with food—dried fruit, jerky, granola, bread, cheese—sleeping bag and pad. He carried three candles and matches but no cooking equipment. No flashlight, no headlamp. No filter pump, no iodine pills for decontaminating water. To hell with giardia. This trip he'd drink directly from cold mountain streams.

"It's an ill wind that blows no good," he reminded himself, lifting and shouldering his pack, checking compression straps, cinching the belt around his waist. It rode comfortably on his hips. Following the cairns that marked the trail, he started away from the lake.

"If I make Blaney Meadows, I won't complain."

He walked slowly but steadily for half an hour, crossing the road to Muir Trail Ranch multiple times. Road and trail were heavily used and eroded, massive lateral roots crisscrossing them, reminding Everett of a Jonah harangue set off by lodgepole pine. Above Yosemite, high in Lyell Canyon, they'd hiked terrain like this, past a hillside of lodgepole flattened in an avalanche.

"Taproots, you *Pinus contorta* idiots! You think laterals are going to anchor you? Get taproots down, you dumb-assed *Murrayana*!" Jonah ranted to the fallen trees, admonishing by genus and species.

"*Murrayana* dumb-assed as ever, Jonah. Nothing has changed."

As young men Everett and Jonah trekked ten miles any day, twenty when they decided to really bust ass, following marked trails when they wanted to make time, striking cross-country when there was a peak or basin they wanted to explore, off-trail their preferred mode.

One afternoon they'd hiked the south fork of the San Joaquin twelve miles out of Goddard Canyon. Arriving Blaney Meadows late, they camped by the river downstream from the dude ranch and stock corral.

The next morning they loitered in camp, writing journal entries, reading. Not much food left but plenty of coffee, and only three miles to the ferry landing. Neither finished the book he'd carried for a week—Jonah, Trotsky's *History of the Russian Revolution*; Everett, *The Autobiography of William Butler Yeats*.

Instead of backtracking to the trail, they headed down canyon to the reservoir. Approaching Florence Lake, they were stopped where the river dropped ten feet. It tore through jumbled boulders, then widened into long, green shallows. She was lying below them on a boulder in the middle of a pool, naked, arms flung wide and hanging over one end of the rock, blonde hair cascading between them, legs spread and dangling over the other end, face, breasts, belly, and pubis stretched taut under the sun. Her lips were parted slightly, her eyes closed. Sunlight glinted off her golden hair and reddish pubic fuzz. Twenty feet above her, they didn't think she'd seen or heard them. The roar of the river would have covered any sound.

They backed off the ledge and cut uphill to go around her. God, she was beautiful, and the way she was lying in the sun was beautiful.

"What does Leon have to say about that?" Everett asked when they could no longer see her and knew she could not hear them.

"Not much," Jonah said. "How about Willie?"

"'Only God, my dear, / Could love you for yourself alone / And not your yellow hair.'"

"I could love her for a lot more than yellow hair," Jonah said.

Everett caught himself talking aloud with Jonah. The day was still, the woods quiet. He'd arrived at the edge of a small meadow, grass turning yellow in late summer. Shadows of trees from behind him were beginning to edge into the clearing. Everett judged it was two o'clock, no later. Without a watch, he'd use shadows to tell time. The trail ran through the glade and into the woods on the other side.

Pain overwhelmed him when he started walking again. He nearly fell, then leaned forward to catch himself. He didn't want to be immobilized here, and waited, the stench of marsh grass rushing into his nostrils. Three or four minutes passed before he could breathe easily and straighten up. It was not just the pain—that was bearable, and he had drugs—but the weakness that always followed, as if a tap opened in his body and energy gushed out. When he was upright again, he crossed the meadow and lowered himself against a tree. He opened his pack, found his medication, placed a Fentanyl under his tongue. Breathing shallowly, he waited for the drug to take hold. Sunlight covered his feet and outstretched legs. A warm breeze brushed his face.

"You don't have to do it this way, Dad," Conrad told him.

"What way?"

"You know what I'm talking about."

"I give up. What are you talking about?"

"I even know where you're going, Dad."

If ever there was a conversation Everett didn't want, it was this one. He wanted to tell Conrad goodbye. One last time, one last hug, and end it like that. It wasn't his to end apparently.

"I'm sorry, Dad. Just leave a note please."

"What?"

"A note. I may think I know where you're going, but you wouldn't have told me, or told anyone, so I wouldn't really know. Do it your way, but I know where you're going."

"Then tell your sister for me."

"You tell Mariah yourself," Conrad said.

So Everett told no one.

He woke still sitting against the tree, branches above him dropping shadows in his lap. Four o'clock, he thought, and then of jumping up and hurrying along. Jumping up was not the way he moved anymore, but move he must. He took two Oxycontin and started.

He hiked for what seemed a long time—to him; he made what seemed like good progress—for him. He felt for the first time he could do what he'd planned. Not just hike four miles to a first camp this evening, but hike the San Joaquin canyon and climb to Evolution Valley. That he'd allowed himself when he started to not feel up to it irritated him. He was too old a hiker to forget you had to get away from the road first, had to get into the country, the same way you had to get out of camp in the morning. No one ever did miles sitting on his ass and wondering how far he'd go that day. You walked your walk or you didn't: it was good he'd got back his walk when he did.

After he got out of the army Laura wanted him to come back to the Midwest. They'd go East, she said, to New England, to Massachusetts, to Boston, to the font of American intellectualism as she saw it, a shrine where, she imagined, thought and reason and all things well thought and well reasoned lay fixed but accessible. She loved her intellectual concepts and meanderings more than any other part of herself, or so she believed, confusing reason for pilotage. So much if not all of how she lived was by dead reckoning, by impulse, temperament, loins, and love—yes, that too.

"Do you love me?" she asked when he called, three weeks before he mustered out, to tell her he was staying in California.

"I love you," he said.

"Then why are you staying in California?"

"Because I want to live here. I love the mountains, deserts, ocean. There are anti-war groups I want to join in Berkeley to protest this stupid war."

"There are anti-war groups in Boston too. I don't want to come to California."

"Why not?"

"I distrust who I might become there, I distrust who you might become. I don't want a casually skimmed existence following fads and impulses. I want a deeply felt, engaged life, and that is more likely to happen in New England than in California."

"You've been reading too much Hawthorne," he'd shouted at her.

"And you've been reading too much Kerouac," she'd answered.

That was telling, telling indeed, he thought, that they'd bandy authors to get at what they wanted and where they wanted to live and how they wanted to love, even knowing they did love each other. Or believed, at least, that they did.

For a year Laura stayed in Ohio, Everett in Berkeley, and they didn't see each other, though they wrote often, called often, quarreled often. He joined stop-the-war groups in Berkeley, started an agitprop troop with students and friends that did shows on sidewalks to raise consciousness of the war—and yes, girls sometimes said "yes" to boys who were saying "no." Everett met Jonah, and they hiked Yosemite and the basins and deserts of California. Laura took a job as administrative assistant to the mayor of a small Ohio city, became enthralled with civic administration, became enthralled too with the mayor. *We travelled together on civic business,* was how she'd later dismiss the affair. One day she left, loaded all her things, seventy percent books, into her 1952 oxidized-green Volkswagen beetle and drove to California.

"You just left?" Everett asked.

"Yes," she said. "He was falling in love with me. I couldn't allow that."

She showed up on an afternoon he'd spent waiting for her. She'd called from Placerville, having driven Highway 50 cross-country. From the window of his house on Grant Street, he watched the old bug pull to the curb and shudder to a stop. She'd found a parking space across the street and emerged from the car wearing a man's blue work shirt and jeans—her workingman's look. Her hair was tied in a messy topknot, her long neck bare. She turned to look first left, then right, but didn't see him standing in the window. When she started across the street, he flung the door open and raced down the steps. Then she was in his arms.

"Let's get inside. Quick," she said.

When he arrived at the trail junction to Muir Trail Ranch, he estimated it was six o'clock. He was pleasantly surprised, pleased with himself; he'd made his first days goal. Striking toward the river to find a campsite for the night, he bumped into the boundary fence for the dude ranch, followed it, heading through tree stumps and new growth for the water. He could hear the river but found himself entangled in underbrush. Skirting the thicket, he moved downstream.

Everett was a backpacking purist. He always picked a slightly sloped flat to bed down in, an area that would drain in a rainstorm. Trenching around a tent was anathema to him, the kind of unnecessary human impact he deplored. Burned rocks in campfire rings irritated him no end. Campfire rings in riparian areas sent him into a fury. He'd spent hours destroying them, removing burnt wood and ashes, burying burnt rocks, smoothing the soil over the fire pit. He was pleased he found no old camps, no remains of fires or flattened vegetation. No one camped this close to Florence Lake; no one camped three miles in. Good grief, he told himself, even if you crossed on the 4:30 ferry, you'd hike past Muir Trail Ranch before you camped.

He was content to be in-country and not collapsed. Working his way downstream, he found a spot he liked within a hundred yards. Rock terraces sloped up from a pool, then gave way to forest where he could spread his sleeping bag. He shed his pack and sat to watch the river. The water level was summer flow, eight to ten feet wide where it tumbled through boulders, then flattened in a pale-green run. A long granite slab sloped into the river as if diving gracefully. Water ouzels darted over the surface, feeding on insects. Everett scooted toward the stream, took off his boots, soaked his feet. He felt good.

Waves rippled up the rock, leaving a wet band that reminded him of human flesh. The earth too was a living organism, wasn't it, susceptible to maladies? The river-wet, rose-tinted granite seemed impervious to decay, but might these rocks develop a deviancy, perhaps begin to reproduce themselves at an alarming rate—massive mountain ranges rising, fracturing the earth's mantle? And in spite of bright sun and blue sky, the planet might weaken, wobble in orbit, drift toward the sun, drift toward oblivion. Impossible but not unimaginable, he thought, imagining it. How fortunate for the planet that rock did not mutate. How calamitous for him that cells did.

He wiggled his toes in the cold water, lifted his feet out, allowed them to dry, then slipped into his boots without socks. When he'd chosen his dinner, he sat again, chewing one raisin at a time, one small broken piece of cheese, one small bit of bread. Sunlight retreated up the gorge like the beam of a slow logging truck, climbing the wall, disappearing. The air was quickly cooler, denser. A nightjar flew up river, gliding from side to side as it passed. A pair of bats scissored after insects on the opposite bank.

"Christ, the world is a beautiful place. Even an insect rises in the evening to drink it in, risking to die. And death in the evening might be beautiful too, a life seized in flight and swallowed whole. I will engorge myself with death, choke on it if I must, chew it like jerky until jaws cease closing. No chance to regurgitate, falling nauseated through all time, dizzy and bilious in endless space. Christ, you're crazy. Oh Christ, yes!"

Evening light was fading. He slipped four Oxycontin in his shirt pocket, then divided his food into two bags and tied them shut. He carried them to a counterbalance line he'd thrown over a tree limb, tied one bag to an end of the line, then hauled it up to the branch. He wrapped the free line in one loop around his shoe and lifted the second food bag. Giving the line slack by raising his foot, he wound the line around the top of the bag as high as he could reach and tied it with double knots, coiled the remaining line in loops, knotted it to the bag. Using his walking stick, he shoved the second bag up to the first, both more than ten feet off the ground, out of reach of bear, raccoon, or mouse. Back to his sleeping bag, he crawled in, lay on his back, gazed at stars.

How many nights had he slept in the open in these mountains? A hundred? Two hundred? Sometimes you paid a price—mosquitoes chewed you all night or a thunderstorm burst at midnight—but for Everett the immense light-spattered sky tipped the balance dramatically against bites and rain.

He woke early, the canyon dark, a small crescent moon and Jupiter a hand's-breadth apart in the west. Pain had awakened him. He fumbled for his Oxycontin, took two capsules, then lay back, shoulders flat, head still, counting each breath, imagining first his feet, then legs, then buttocks relaxing into the ground. Venus had risen, a tiny spark on the horizon, and he remembered other mornings, waking in the mountains at predawn, Venus a pinprick of light in the eastern sky.

The summer Laura and Kate hiked the John Muir trail for a week, he and Randy—Kate's significant other—made plans to meet them in Evolution Valley. They drove all night, having left late after a baseball game and a few pints at the pub, arriving Florence Lake at four in the morning. Out of the car in false dawn, Everett argued with Randy to wait for the first ferry at 8:30 to save five miles of a twenty-mile hike.

"No way," Randy insisted, and they'd started on the long slog around the lake, arriving at the trailhead other side Florence Lake at 7.

"Saved two hours with five easy miles," Randy bragged.

"Hour and a half. First ferry gets here at 8:30."

"Leaves the store at 8:30. Has to cross the lake before it gets here."

"Doesn't take a half hour to cross the lake. Maybe ten minutes."

"Okay, saved an hour forty minutes with an easy five miles."

"They won't seem easy come five o'clock this afternoon. You'll see."

And see they did. After force-marching four miles to Blaney Meadows, they took a short break, then hiked to Piute Creek. After a long break for lunch—Everett trying to nap, Randy pacing anxiously—they charged on into the afternoon, the trail steeper now, Piute Creek to Evolution Creek, and at last the climb up the wall into Evolution Valley. They approached the top in the evening, opening and closing the drift fence at the last narrows in the trail. Laura had been waiting and sprinted down the trail toward them, her long hair lifting behind her. Her face was tanned and glowing, her dark eyes sparkling. Everett watched her bound toward him, startled by the sheer animal beauty of this woman, his wife, galvanized by her week's hiking. Her face radiant, she cried, "I love you!"

before flinging herself into him. "I missed you," he said. And she, "Me too." And he, "You're beautiful. You're stunning." And she, "Oh God, I love you."

Christ, it happened such a long time ago, Everett thought, comfortable now, medication working, in his sleeping bag by the San Joaquin, never taking his eye off Venus but seeing Laura rushing toward him again, aroused by the memory, wanting her terribly in that moment by the river under the morning stars.

In the dark, he could hear the slap of water against rock, the tug and rush of current moving past boulders. Could smell wet rock and soaked roots hanging from dank earth. After a time, could see the river. A pale, ethereal morning light glazed its pools and rapids.

II

Everett rose in semi-darkness and rolled up his sleeping bag. There was no dew. He hooked into the rope securing the food cache with his walking stick and pulled everything down. Taking out two granola bars, he stowed the food bags and rope in his backpack. In ten minutes he was ready and retraced his route along the Muir Trail Ranch boundary fence and back onto the trail.

He set his mind to the task he'd set his body, gauging every twitch or tic in every muscle. Tension in the right calf? He favored it immediately. In fifty steps, the tension disappeared. His backpack rode easily on his shoulders. He shifted the weight to hips, shifted it to shoulders again. His body felt fine surprisingly. A controlled next step, and a next, and another. Satisfied, he walked steadily for thirty minutes before he began to tire, estimating he'd gone more than a mile. Should he push himself? The morning was still early. Better to rest often and husband strength—or better to hike to exhaustion? Weakness was the problem, not pain. His strength would suddenly vanish, fatigue overwhelm him. There was nothing he could do about it.

"To hell with the pain, Jonah. What I need is an opiate for weakness!"

"Don't be shocked. I'm thinner than you've ever seen me. I'm below what I weighed in high school," Jonah had warned him.

"What's going on?"

"I'll tell you when we have lunch Thursday."

Jonah—tall, gaunt, pallid—walked in using a cane, opening the door wide before he stepped through. He wasn't tottering, but in his slow, careful steps Everett no longer saw the jaunty bounce he'd envied in Jonah's walk. He locked eyes with Everett and smiled.

"I knew you'd be shocked, Everett. I told you."

"You're a little thin. Yeah, you said that."

They ordered sandwiches, sat outside. The midday sun was burning off the Berkeley morning fog.

"I've been dealt some pretty shitty cards this time," Jonah said.

"How bad?"

"Pancreatic cancer."

"Holy shit."

He wished he'd said something more meaningful. He thought their years of friendship deserved more than "holy shit," but Jonah smiled wanly as if he'd expected little more.

"They did an exploratory. It's everywhere. They can't treat it, they say, unless they rip my insides out. Six months, a year at most."

"You don't have to be stoic with me."

"I'm not being stoic. Whining about it won't change anything. Live while you can, then let go."

"Are you in pain?"

"I'm on drugs. I know the pain's there, but I'm on drugs."

Everett had to stop. His leg muscles were rebelling—not rebelling, but ceasing to function. He'd wanted to postpone resting until he'd bagged two miles, but there was no going on.

Why should it matter? He wasn't going anywhere. He had a destination but no time limit, no date to get anywhere. He'd left time behind at the ferry landing. He imagined it a ball of steel springs tightly rolled and compressed—residue of strategies he'd once owned hardened to metal strips, fused remnant schemes and expectations left weathering in the Sierra sun. Metal fragments flew off the ball as it decayed, the mass expanding and fracturing simultaneously, time letting go as he'd let time go.

"I'm letting go, Everett," Jonah said. "Letting the least things go: the wars, the histories, what had seemed inherently critical social and societal issues and patterns of human development and strife. They seem of no concern now. They don't interest me now."

"What does?"

"Family. My wife, Ellen. My son, Marcus. Ellen has a cousin who plays guitar. He lives two blocks away and comes to play for me. I sit and listen. I'd never have done that before. I had no patience. I was obsessed with things."

"'Waves of anger and fear/...Obsessing our private lives,' as Auden wrote."

"That's it. Anger and fear don't obsess anymore, but poetry does. I've been reading and memorizing. Do you know the poem 'Mind of Winter'?"

"'One must have a mind of winter.' Yes, 'The Snowman.' Stevens."

"I've memorized that poem. It seems as important as anything to me now. 'One must have a mind of winter/...not to think/of any misery in the sound of the wind.' I think he's talking about death."

"I'm not so sure. I think he's talking about a way of seeing. Perhaps learning to think of the thing itself, not how you experience it."

"Yes."

"And is it misery?"

"Not so much. You find a way not to think of the misery in it. We're all going to die. I just know when. In some ways it's better, except for the unfinished, or what you believe is unfinished. But you can let the unfinished go too."

"What's the unfinished for you?"

"My grandchildren. I will miss their excitements, their successes. I'd like to go to the high country once more, sit on the granite, wake one more morning among the Sierra peaks. I can't hike anymore. I'll have to let that go."

"I can take you."

"I can't hike anymore, Everett."

"You won't have to. We'll go to Saddlebag Lake, to the walk-in campground along Lee Vining Creek a hundred yards from the car. Anyone can get in there."

"I don't want to be carried in."

"No one has to carry you. They have those flat wooden wheelbarrows for hauling gear into campsites. We'll lay you belly down on a wheelbarrow and roll you in. It'll give you a new perspective of the mountains."

"I'd like that. A new perspective. We'll have to see."
"See what?"
"What do you think? See what shape I'm in."

Midday was approaching before Everett was hiking again. The sun was overhead, shining directly into the sparse groves he passed through, though it was not terribly hot. Warm breezes were beginning to rise from the valley, mountain air cooling valley air as they mingled.

After Senger Creek, the trail paralleled the canyon wall fifty to a hundred yards above the river, climbing gently with the contour of the valley. Everett set himself a milestone—the conifer with a broken branch in its crown—and hiked toward it at a steady pace, one foot in front of the other. Dust rose from each footstep, settling on his toes. "Dust and boots, dust and boots," he chanted, establishing a cadence that propelled his walking. "Dust and boots. Boots and dust."

A group of hikers who must have crossed on the 8:30 ferry passed him, hustling along, talking loudly. Young, young and noisy. He heard them long before they overtook him and moved a few steps off the trail to allow them to go by. Each greeted him boisterously but none really paid him attention. None slowed as they hurried by, and they were soon gone, passing the milestone conifer in minutes, or so it seemed. He stepped back onto the trail, marveling at the pace they kept in the midday sun.

"'Mad dogs and Englishmen go out in the midday sun.' And the young. Coward, you old reprobate. You missed the young!" he shouted.

"'Mad dogs and Englishmen,' and the young, and the young."

He marched in cadence, step and step with the mad dogs, step and step in the midday sun, step and step with the young. When he reached and passed the conifer, he picked another milestone: the rock outcrop upstream where the trail dropped toward the river.

Time was no longer measured in seconds, minutes, hours. Time had become his capacity for endurance, calibrated in molecules of oxygen arriving in the cells of his calves and thighs, arriving in his heart, brain, will. How much oxygen did his will need? There hardly seemed enough. Maybe so little oxygen was arriving in his aberrant cells their metastasis was also slowed. Maybe he could walk himself into health by exhausting those bastards, starving the *fuckers,* burning the body alive from the inside out. Maybe there was a method to mad dogs. Tramp, tramp in the midday sun. Tramp, and push on.

What the hell did Coward know about mad dogs? Or midday sun? How often had he ever been near going out midday? Had Kipling written the ditty? Kipling would know mad dogs, know midday sun, but Everett was pretty sure the verse belonged to Coward.

"Coward, Kipling. Kipling, Coward." Another cadence for walking. Two steps with Coward, two with Kipling. Hiking with ghosts.

He passed the rock outcrop and stopped in a copse of lodgepole, where in the rainy season a creek flowed. The creek was dry now, stones in it baked and whitened. Eddies of small gravel lay like grain where they'd swirled in pools and dried. Reeds that had thrived in the spring were brown and tottering. Everett plopped down, exhausted.

Everett's desk at the rocket propulsion plant was vintage steelcase Tanker, basic military issue, white Formica top browning at the corners. Light dropped through dust motes from fixtures high in the converted production building. Everyone complained about how poorly the work area was lighted.

"You are here as contractors," Tom, the project leader, said. "Make the best of it."

An aerospace engineer, Tom had allowed himself to be promoted into quality and project management positions, roles that left him uncomfortable because he didn't control engineering input. He never completely trusted mechanical engineers.

"They'll do anything to make a widget work," he liked to say, "but sometimes the anything is not sustainable."

"Keep an eye on everything," he told Everett when they'd become confidants. "Any meeting you attend, anything you see—let me know about it."

Josie was a training specialist on Tom's team. She and Everett shared the same office, the same projects. She had filmed a nozzle installation training video scripted by the project engineer, Dave, and Everett was assigned to accompany her to review it for Tom. They met with Dave in a small conference room. In the video, a worker unpacked a graphite seal, applied adhesive, aligned the seal with thumb screws, then tightened the fixture to allow the seal to bond. Though Dave pronounced the video excellent, the whole process looked shoddy to Everett.

"Why are we bonding the nozzle seal manually if it's the most critical step?"

"If the fixture is properly aligned, the seal will be properly bonded," Dave said.

"But the fixture has to be manually aligned. Not good. What are the controls for this adjustment? It has to be done correctly, doesn't it?"

"Who the fuck are you, the tech writer, telling me how to engineer the nozzle seal bond?"

"I'm not telling you anything. I'm saying this step should be Murphy-proofed if it's critical. That's simple quality oversight, not engineering."

"You're a fucking tech writer, not the QA."

"Who the hell do you think I work for? Tom is the director of QA!"

"But you're not Tom, you miserable little scrivener!" Dave yelled, storming out.

"Wow," Everett marveled aloud, laughing. "Have to hand it to Dave, reaching back in his vocabulary to find *scrivener*. Not bad for an engineer."

Josie said nothing. She switched off the projector, and the room was quiet. As Everett gathered his notes into a neat stack, he could hear pages slide past each other; his tapping the stack on the table seemed deafening. He turned to find Josie watching him.

"What should I do with this video?" Josie asked. "I gather you won't take it to Tom."

"Of course we'll take it to Tom. It will help explain what's wrong with it. The concept is flawed."

"There's nothing wrong with the training material, is there?"

"The video is fine. The process is wrong."

"Can you please make that clear to Tom?"

"Yes, of course. What are you saying?"

"Sweetie," she said—she'd never called him Sweetie before—"don't critique me out of a job please."

He blushed, and was surprised he blushed. The intensity with which she watched him unsettled him.

"Don't worry," he said, reaching toward her, intending to pat her hand. "I will not scrap the boat with the barnacles."

She took his hands, first in one of hers, then both, and he drew her slowly toward him. Faces inches apart, they remained that way for what seemed to Everett forever, a small wonderful forever in a small conference room in a converted production hangar. When he relaxed his hands, she pulled away, the tips of her fingers flowing off his skin.

"This is crazy," she said.

"We'll go see Tom," he said. "This is something we can all discuss."

"Yes," she said. "Yes."

Why was he sitting in this dried creek bed? No water, no view. Piute Creek was his goal, but Piute Creek wasn't coming to him.

"So suck it up, ye old bones. We have trail to trod."

On his way again, the exhortations to his bones had little effect. Each footstep seemed a discrete act that floundered toward rather than flowed into walking. He pushed himself along, charging his feet to carry him, counting each step an accomplishment.

A pack train from Florence Lake overtook him, the creak of harnesses and pounding of steel-shod mules loud. When he moved off the trail to let them pass, the drover nodded his thanks, and then they were past.

Everett hated pack trains: hoofed trail destroyers humping supplies for campers unwilling to hike. There were few things he hated more than a fat ass rocking past him, rider smiling knowingly as if he or she shared the same experience of the great outdoors as he. Hardly! He shuddered that he was doomed to share the trail with them; he was determined to never camp with them. He'd find a secluded spot past Piute Creek where no one would camp nearby, a site where no one would stumble onto him. That was his promise to himself.

He tried to lengthen each step, tried to capture a cadence that would increase his pace. "Piute Creek—step, step, STEP. Piute Creek—step, step, STEP." Unable to drive his feet to match his chant, he slowed to a shuffle.

"Don't want an occurrence at Piute Creek Bridge. Don't want to be carried out in a Human Remains Pouch. No HRPs at Shiloh, none at Gettysburg, certainly none at Owl Creek."

The trail climbed steeply to the narrow gorge and bridge. Everett stepped onto the wooden deck and leaned against the railing. The creek ran clear and shallow below him, no more than a foot deep, rocks in the streambed raising small rapids. Everett imagined dipping hands into the water, savoring its chill, a cold mouthful flowing down his throat. He stood still and rested; in time he'd climb down to the stream.

Sensation fascinated Laura, not just the excitation of the moment, the pain or joy, but the implanting of it in memory. When Mariah was due, she looked forward to childbirth, she said. Couldn't wait, she said, for labor to begin.

"Are you crazy?"

"What is there to fear?"

"It is generally held to be painful."

"How would you know?"

"It's not necessarily classified information."

"I expect to enjoy it," she said.

Giving birth, she screamed furiously and wide-mouthed, crushing Everett's hands, yanking herself toward him with each contraction. Everett shouted at her, "Goddamn it! Breathe!" She screamed to everyone to get her out of there, to stop the pain, to kill her if they had to, wave after violent wave of screaming full volume that went on for hours. Then the baby came. A loud scream turned into a long, triumphant trill, then morphed to cooing as she reached for her baby. Wide-eyed and lifting Mariah to her breasts, she shouted, "My God, that was incredible!"

He looked at his hands where they rested on the railing, hands bruised for days after Mariah's birth. Wonderfully bruised, he'd thought at the time.

How fascinating hands by design grasp, yet let go so easily, let go so easily of so much. Laura described giving birth as being wonderfully, completely at the mercy of nature. How was that different from any other day or moment? Any breath taken is wonderfully, completely at the mercy of nature, isn't it? Grasping is completely at the mercy of nature, letting go too. The things you pick up, the things you drop. All completely at the mercy of nature, no? The testosterone-ladened lad's mad pursuit, the maid's yielding—all wonderfully, completely at the mercy of nature, aren't they?

Another three hikers were coming up the trail, their chatter loud above the roar of Piute Creek. Anxious not to be seen, Everett hurried across the bridge, left the trail, cut downslope. The hillside was littered with boulders he climbed around awkwardly. He scrambled toward the river, down the crumbling wall of shelves and rock faces. When the sound of the hikers was lost, he slipped his pack and flopped down against it.

This was not a good place. Getting to water wouldn't be easy. However, it was the kind of spot no one else was likely to find, which pleased Everett. He could shelter here. There were level spaces between trees, depressions filled with fallen needles and pine cones, room enough for a sleeping bag. He didn't need a good camp. He just needed rest.

White water poured through the river below him, lifted in a blue wave by a boulder. The wave dropped, swept against the bank, slowed, then formed a clear, still pool while the current shot by inches away. He watched the water, gazing from crest to crest. After a time his eyes moved without his directing them, each wave drawing them to find another part of the stream. He was content to let his eyes lead, to watch, to rest, to drift.

They arrived Wishon Reservoir noon and struck out for Blackcap Basin, destination for the first day Woodchuck Lake. The climb out of the canyon was arduous. They rested often and watched clouds drift up from the valley. By midafternoon the clouds weren't drifting but driven by a rising wind. Hikers coming out of the high country—and there were many—paused to warn them a storm was forecast. Several suggested they turn back.

"Are we going to be all right?" Laura asked.

"Don't see why not. How serious can a storm in June be anyway?"

"They seem to think it's going to be serious. And it looks pretty serious. I don't see any break in those clouds."

"We have a good tent, good sleeping bags, food, camp stove, fuel. What do we care if a storm hits?"

By late afternoon the sun disappeared and clouds began to mass against the peaks above the basin. The temperature had begun to drop by the time they made Woodchuck Lake. They pitched their tent in a copse of twisted pines back from the lake, then gathered firewood to heat water. Wind laid the flames flat; what little heat was generated swept off into the evening. After the pot sat on the fire half an hour, water still not warm, Everett lit the camping stove to boil it. The lake's surface was washboarded, ruffled, whitecapped by the wind.

By dusk a fine rain was falling. The two ends of rope he'd anchored from a branch swayed in the wind. He hung their food and shoved their gear into the tent.

"Did you check there's no food in those backpacks?" Laura asked.

"I don't think we have to worry. 'It ain't a fit night out for man or beast.'"

"But what if no one told the beasts?"

"The wind tells them; God tells them. They have an ear for that 'still small voice.'"

"You'd blaspheme on a night like this?"

"I have the calm confidence of a Christian with a mountain tent and two down sleeping bags. Get in here."

They stacked the packs against the sides of the tent and spread the sleeping bags—zippered together into one wide sack—on pads in the middle, then snuggled in, chatting about how comfortable their nest, remembering and sharing a story of John Muir supposedly dancing all night on a glacier to keep warm. "Muir never carried a sleeping bag?" she asked. — "Only a blanket." They wondered if Mrs. Muir ever went with John. He remembered she had once, to Yosemite Valley. "They must have had a tent then." — "They stayed in a cabin." — "How do you know?" — "He wrote about it."

They bantered about whether the Muirs enjoyed camping together as much as they, doubted they had. "How could they? They couldn't read. They never had headlamps." — "John Muir never had a headlamp?" — "Of course not." — "And they were an old married couple." — "What's wrong with an old married couple?" — "I'm waiting to see," she said.

The wind died down after midnight. The night was quiet, so quiet he woke, so quiet he could hear Laura breathing in the dark where she lay snuggled against his shoulder. He kissed her face; she didn't waken. Confident the worst of the storm had passed, he fell asleep again.

When he woke at daylight and peeked out, a white world greeted him. The ground was covered with three inches of snow, and more was coming down—thick wet spring snow falling steadily. Not the slightest breeze. Just the snow falling quietly: huge flakes dropping like gull feathers into the dark lake, disappearing instantly when they touched water. The snow stuck to boulders, rimming the lake with a white collar. It covered every branch of the scrub pine trees scattered among the boulders. It had not yet covered the sedge grasses at the shallow upper edges of the lake. Flakes continued to fall, disappearing among grass stems as if the snow understood its next task was to whiten these.

"What are we going to do?" Laura asked.

"I think we'll stay in the tent and let it snow."

"I can't. I have to pee."

"Me too. And I have to get the food down."

Bladders relieved, food in hand, they spent the day in the tent reading. Laura, *The World as I Found It.* A novel about Wittgenstein, five hundred pages. "Five hundred pages on Wittgenstein? Is that possible?" he asked. "It's not just Wittgenstein. Bertrand Russell and George Moore too." — "The more philosophers, the more pages I suppose." — "It's not just philosophy. It's their lives, their loves." —"Russell had a reputation: the priapic sage." — "I haven't read that far yet," she said.

"Let's get priapic."

"I can't. It applies to men. From Priapus, the Roman god of fertility."

"Oh come on. You can do priapic. I know you can."

"Read your book," she said.

Everett, *Lonesome Dove.* Cowboy epic, eight hundred pages. "Lots of roping and shooting, I imagine," she said. — "I expect so." — "And epic male camaraderie I bet." — "I imagine there will be." — "And occasional priapic behavior too, I assume." — "I haven't read that far yet," he said.

They read, they talked. Ate nuts and cheeses and snacks for breakfast. Ate nuts and cheeses and snacks for lunch. They snuggled in the down bags, made love slowly, patiently, then read again. The morning passed.

They avoided bumping the roof of the tent, which collected condensation. They unzipped the tent door and, side by side, sat in front of it wrapped in their bedding, watching the snow fall.

"It's not that cold," she said.

"It's June."

"The solstice is tomorrow. And we're watching it snow."

"It won't last."

By midafternoon the snow stopped. By four o'clock the sun broke through, showering the basin with warmth. Branches began to drip water. Where sunbeams struck a rock, snow melted quickly and the rock steamed. Water puddled as the snow retreated, rivulets pouring from slopes into the lake. Their tent was on high ground, but the soil under it became soggy. They moved out and sat in sunlight on a drying rock near the lake.

"I'm going to bathe," she said.

"You are what?"

"Heat me a bit of water. I stink."

"I love the way you smell."

"A quart, that's all I need."

He found the camp stove, brought it out to the lake, lit it. The afternoon was still; the hiss of burning gas seemed to roar through the basin. They listened, then started to laugh, amused by the tiny gadget fizzing noisily into the still, water-dripping afternoon.

"It sounds as if it's about to take off," she said. "It's called a Pocket Rocket," he said, sending them into another round of laughter. "Pocket rockets! Headlamps! How much technology are we carrying?" — "Don't forget the water pump." — "What would hiking be without backcountry filtration?" — "Or backcountry bathing, for that matter."— "You'll appreciate it later," she said.

When the water was warm, she stripped. Winding her hair into a loose bun and using the one small towel they carried, she wiped leisurely around her neck, her face, savoring warmth in the cloth. Everett watched her raise each hand and arm into the blue sky, then wipe underarms, breasts, stomach, thighs. When she finished, he rubbed her briskly with a dry T-shirt. She slipped back into her clothes and leaned against him, sitting on the rock.

Euphoria swept over him—a mixture of excitement, contentment, exultation. The overwhelming trust that filled him at that moment dazzled him. He buried his face in Laura's hair, breathing deeply, then deeply again.

"What're you doing?" she asked.

"Being happy," he said.

And he was: he'd compare that afternoon with any of his life, with any afternoon of anyone's life. Just Laura, the warm granite, the lake, the white snow-dappled basin, the blue dome of the sky, the patter of snowmelt falling from tree branches, falling from grasses and bushes, falling from granite ledges in the bright late-afternoon sun, and the edgy whisper of mountain wind making its way upcanyon as the water made its way down.

III

When Everett woke, he was still sitting against his pack. His first thought was he'd slept all night; morning had come and he could be off hiking. If he could move. His legs were stiff and achy, and something jabbed like a bayonet at his kidneys. Twisting across to his backpack, he dug for his Fentanyl, shaking a handful of pills into his palm. Popping two under his tongue, he shoved his pack aside. The pack struck his water bottle, which toppled over, bounced off a rock, rolled downhill. Scrambling, he grabbed the bottle before it caromed into the river but dropped most of the Fentanyl pills. One hand grasping water bottle, the other closed on pills, he lay on his side coaxing himself to breathe normally as pain wracked his body.

Five minutes! "Goddamn it!" Ten minutes! "Jesus Christ!" Fifteen minutes! "Please, God!" The pain began to ease. Finally he could breathe, take in lungsful of air, feel a tentative confidence in controlling his body. With the help of a drug—but control was better than anarchy no matter how achieved.

Pain relieved, he turned on his back and watched white clouds drift upriver against blue sky. It occurred to him they knifed through the sky the way pain slashed through his body. It didn't seem anything as buoyant as clouds could slice through space, but who was to say mutant cells savaging his organs might not appear buoyant to some sentient cell inside an intestine wall unaware of the damage caused by their winding through him. Who's to say?

"I'm to say, damn it. Let no schmuck tell me it's all perception. I know better," Everett grumbled, but then wasn't sure he did know. The billowy clouds continued to drift upcanyon.

On hands and knees, he hunted through stones and twigs for the pills he'd dropped, picking them up one by one. Storing two in his shirt pocket, he slipped the others in the pack, then hobbled along the slope checking for a spot to spend the night. He chose one that didn't tip downhill and dropped his gear, confident he could sleep there without rolling into the river.

Crisscrossing the hillside, he found a tree to hang his food. The branch where he suspended a line wasn't ten feet out from the trunk, but the slope dropped away steeply. It would do.

Needing water, he headed for the creek instead of the river. Less coyote shit, he reasoned. Certainly less horseshit. He worked his way across the hill until he stood above the ravine where the creek thundered through. Upstream he found a break in the bank and scrambled down. He was far enough below the footbridge he could not see it. He filled his canteen, drank, filled the canteen again, retraced his steps to his camp. Choosing food, he perched on his pack and ate, chewing, marking time, as evening came on.

Everyone on the satellite launch project met for lunch last work day of the week at the steak house on Sunrise Boulevard. On Friday Josie arranged for Everett to pick her up at home. Her car was in the shop for maintenance, her-four-year old daughter, Teddy, with her ex-husband.

When she opened the door, she was barefoot and wearing a loose-fitting robe. "I'm not ready yet. I'll hurry," she said, grabbing his hand, pulling him through the doorway. The door closed. They said nothing. His hands found her body inside the robe.

Afterward, they lay on the rumpled bed, gazing at each other, silent. She stroked his chest, running her fingertips around his nipples, tweezing his chest hair.

"We're missing lunch," he said.

She began to laugh, really laugh.

"What's so funny?"

"We're going to miss a lot of lunches, Sweetie."

Damn it, Jonah, I got what I wanted from life, or thought I did. I used to wonder if you got what you wanted. I'd say, "No, he didn't. He didn't want to die that soon." Who would?

We're used to living. We live twenty-two, twenty-five, thirty thousand days. One day we're told we have two hundred or three hundred left, plus or minus ten percent. Then we die. Twenty to thirty thousand days for living, one for dying. We get used to knowing we're going to die; we don't get used to dying.

"They want to make it easier for me," Jonah said. "And I want to make it easier for them. I think everything starts there.

"I find it strange sometimes they're grieving. I'm busy—how can I say it?—putting things away. Yes, putting thoughts away, putting ideas away. I want to divest myself of thinking.

"But everyone is watching and listening, collecting what I divest, collecting words, things they want to remember. Jonah said this; Jonah said that. What are they going to do with those, Everett? Why do you think they want them?"

"Is that a rhetorical question?"

"No."

"They want them to remember you by when you're gone."

"Yes, my body's fading. My mind comes and goes. I'm on drugs. You know that, right?"

"Yes."

"I try to imagine my last lucid thought. What'll it be? I think of it as an object, a piece of driftwood perhaps, something I could gift wrap and give to Ellen and say, 'Here's my last thought. I'm finished now.' And the one before last I'd wrap and give Marcus, and the third to last I'd give Artie."

"And which last thought would I get?"

"Nothing for you, Everett. You get this blather. That's all." And they both laughed.

But it's not like that, Jonah; you knew it, and I know it. As long as you live, it's all about living. It's about "I'm hungry now." About "Are you thinking about Jonah again?" "Are you thinking about Laura, Mariah, Conrad, Josie?" It's about "Have you hung the goddamn food? Get your ass up. It's getting dark."

Hard to get my ass up anymore, Jonah. Damned hard.

IV

Everett's goal third day was the junction where the Muir Trail forked, one branch into Goddard Canyon, the main trail up the wall into Evolution Valley. Four miles, easy enough, he thought, lying in his sleeping bag in early-morning darkness, but he wasn't confident. *Easy* seemed to fall away from every task he attached it to like a name tag that had lost its adhesive.

At first light he packed, filled his canteen at the creek, shouldered his backpack, and started. The climb soon turned ugly. Scrambling down the evening before had not been difficult; now the hillside seemed steeper. Boulders he hadn't noticed the day before blocked his passage. Gooseberry bushes grew thick between rock piles, hampering his getting around them. When his walking stick stuck in brushwood, he fell sideways, catching himself against a boulder with left forearm and elbow, head banging hard against rock.

He lay still until his head stopped throbbing, then reached back to check his ear. His hand came away with blood. His left forearm was scraped from wrist to elbow, blood beading where skin was lacerated.

"You blocks, you stones, you worse than senseless things!" he moaned, pushing himself up, grabbing his walking stick. He tugged, but it didn't come loose and toppled away from him.

"All right, I don't need you."

Finding a bandana, he dabbed at the ear and arm. Neither hurt much. He'd taken drugs before he'd started. The drugs were good for pain, and he loved them for that, but they made him lightheaded. Bloodied and dizzy, he was prostrate an hour before sunrise.

"A gorgeous start today, Jonah. You can't imagine."

Five minutes passed before he managed to retrieve the walking stick, bracing one hand on the boulder, snatching the stick with the second, then seizing the hand grip with the first. Pulling with both hands, he freed it, slid off the boulder, and fought his way uphill out of the brush he'd been entangled in. He moved laterally into scattered lodgepole, climbing slowly. Striking the trail a few hundred yards past Piute Creek, he turned east, but stopped within a few steps.

He hated being tired, every muscle resisting commands to keep moving. For God's sake, it was early morning. All his life he'd been an early riser, waking full of energy, ready to roll.

Laura was like him. Most days she was off to the gym by six.

"Why do you do it?"

"I have to stay in shape or you won't want me anymore."

"I'll always want you," Everett said.

Most mornings after she left, he puttered around the house, sometimes fixing a light breakfast of toast and cereal, sometimes squeezing orange juice. He'd leave a glass on the kitchen counter for Laura, covering it with a saucer and adding a note: an x for a kiss perhaps, a set of lips, a heart. Conrad was still asleep. A senior in high school, he was rarely seen out of his room before the last five minutes he had to leave for class. Mariah was already at UC Santa Barbara. Everett would dress, leave the house, and drive the ten miles to work.

In the car—often before he'd even pulled away from the curb—he'd start thinking about Josie, anxious to see her. He liked that he usually arrived before her; he liked watching her come in. She didn't just walk into a room: she floated in, green eyes flaring, red hair flying, always smiling. On the freeway, he'd imagine her getting up, hustling her daughter out of bed, showering, the habit she had of bowing her head, neck arched forward, as she dried her hair. He'd picture her looking into the mirror, lining her eyes, smiling to check the effect. When he arrived at the office, he'd stand by Josie's desk if no one was in, sometimes swivel her chair, sometimes sit in it, all the time joyous she would be with him for the day.

He'd walked again and stopped again, not sucking air but needing rest. How could anyone be so weak and not even be out of breath? There was no logic to it, but no getting out of it. He was determined this morning not to rest until he'd made it halfway to the Evolution Valley cutoff. At least halfway. When he sat, a breather too often turned into a long break. So he stood, waiting to recover enough to go on.

The trail after Piute Creek ran close to the river. In some sections a thin band of trees grew between trail and river, but rock usually rimmed the water. He'd never liked this section of trail. Before he'd hurried through it without much thought. It pained him his passage today would be slow and tedious, unvaried, unrelieved.

"There's no hurry left in me."

He waited, poked at the rocks at his feet, started again. One step, two steps, he drove himself forward, trying to find a chant to support his pace. Maybe a dirge this morning. "The fourth, the fifth, the minor fall, the major lift." He could remember snatches of lyrics—"Hallelujah!" "You needed proof"—but couldn't remember how Cohen fit them together. Everett used them as best he could. Step with the minor fall. Step with the major lift. Something about her beauty overthrew you. There wasn't much cadence he could find in that.

When they met at Josie's house for lunch, they'd rush into the bedroom, grabbing for each other, getting out of shirt, blouse, pants quickly, laying them carefully atop each other on the hope chest. No wrinkles when back to the office. He loved to drop to his knees and pull her naked body to him, running his hands up her thighs. Long legs, long woman, long love overthrew him.

"And you never thought of it as cheating on Laura?"

"I didn't, Jonah. Having Josie made me love Laura more."

"You've got to be kidding."

"No, seriously. Each was a wonder unto herself. I never thought of Josie when I held Laura, never thought of Laura when I held Josie. Laura was *my forever*, Josie *my joie de vivre*. Neither diminished the other. How could I let go of either?"

"'The only thing I cannot resist is temptation,' Wilde warned us. You had better listen."

"It's not like that, Jonah. I love them both. Still do. I can't let either go."

"Your logic may not hold either."

"I'm not so sure. I said to Josie once, 'Why don't you ask me to leave Laura? Why have you never asked for that?'

"'Because I believe you love her. I believe you've always loved her,' she said.

"'Do you believe I love you?'

"'Yes, I believe you love me,' she said. 'And I love you.'"

Drained, feeling ancient, he leaned hard on his walking stick, eyes fixed on broken bits of rock in his path, glacial till from the ice age. He imagined following the first beasts after the glaciers started to melt, cavorting with them, his step light and unflagging, his feet companions to all feet following the melting ice. Horses' hooves, the mastodons' toes. The glacier melted. The canyon opened, walls bare, stark, unflowered, untreed, shaved clean by ice. Horses and mastodons vanished. The grief Everett felt for their passing astonished him as he rested, imagining the ice retreating, the river materializing, the trail materializing beside it. He wanted so much to go on but had no strength.

Hikers came up quickly behind him, before he could move off the trail: two boys, two women, all carrying packs and hiking briskly. A fishing pole was stuck like a radio antenna in each boy's pack; they passed him without speaking. The women slowed and greeted him as they approached, then stopped, boys waiting on the trail ahead.

One woman was stocky, compact, a Patagonia cap pulled down tight over her forehead. The other was broad shouldered and freckled, sandy brown hair escaping in curls from under a wide brimmed sun hat.

"Are you okay?" the woman in the sun hat asked.

"Yes. YES," Everett said, startled by the question. "I'm okay."

"You don't look okay. You have blood on your neck."

"I'm fine. I just hit a rock."

"He says he's okay, Julie," the stocky woman said.

"I don't think he's okay," Julie said. "You look sick."

"I'm not sick. I'm out here, aren't I?"

"Doesn't mean you should be. Are you alone?"

"No, my family's up ahead. I fell behind."

"His family's with him," the stocky woman said.

"Okay," Julie said.

They walked on, much to Everett's relief, but paused again where the boys were waiting. Summoning his strength, Everett started walking as fast as he could to show he was fine. It was hard enough to walk, let alone to walk fast simply to impress people watching him.

Eventually he caught up to them. Julie had opened her pack and taken out a first-aid kit. She blocked his getting past.

"I'm going to dress that wound," she said.

"Oh God," the stocky woman groaned. The boys looked on, amused.

"No," Everett said. "I'm okay."

"You're not okay."

"I have people out here. They'll help me. Who are you anyway?"

"I'm an emergency room nurse. Sit down."

She had authority. There didn't seem much point arguing. She helped Everett shed his pack, lifted it off his shoulders, put it down, pointed for him to sit on it. Kneeling beside him, she swabbed his ear and neck with alcohol.

"You have quite a bruise."

"I'm okay."

"The ear's split. You must have whacked yourself hard."

"I'm okay."

"I'm covering this with a butterfly bandage. You might want a suture or two when you get back. How long you in for?"

"A few days."

"Keep it taped tight. You don't want it to scab and heal split before you get out."

"I'll be okay."

"You look like you can barely go on. Why would your family leave you like this?"

"They know I'll catch up. I'm fine."

"He's fine, Julie," the stocky woman said. "Let's go."

When they were gone, Everett felt terrified: he was exposed on the trail. Hikers would come downriver at him; hikers would come upriver to overtake him. He couldn't imagine anyone worse than this Julie, who'd bullied her way to dress his ear. Jesus Christ, how good a nurse was she? What kind of medical term was *sick*? But he knew he looked emaciated, so others might notice. Some might ask questions. He didn't want to be noticed; he didn't want to be questioned. If hiking before sunrise hadn't shielded him, what would midday be like? What would afternoon be like? An animal traveled in early morning and late evening. He had to think like an animal.

A lizard darted onto a rock. Everett watched it, not moving, waiting, envying. Lizards traveled light, lizards scurried, lizards dashed about. He was far past dashing about, so there was little value thinking like a lizard. A better model might be a tick. If he could think like a tick and find some living organism to crawl onto, he could be carried to Evolution Valley. He could toss the backpack and ride. Where were those mastodons who'd never roamed the Sierra Nevada? Didn't even have to be a mastodon. Any Pleistocene critter would do.

He felt listless and leaden but challenged himself to move. Had three miles to go. Had to get up off his pack; wasn't going to get anywhere sitting on his ass. He still intended to camp at the Evolution Valley trail junction.

V

For their first anniversary, Josie gave him a volume of poems by Villon. In a hotel at a seminar they attended in Los Angeles, she lay in bed beside him reading the poems in French.

"Me vint ung vouloir de brisier / La tres amoureuse prison / Quo souloit mon cuer debrisier."

"Something about prison," he said. "What is that?"

"He's promising himself to break out of the prison of love. *Tres amoureuse*: very in love, very loving."

"And do you find me very loving?"

"I do," she said. "It's translated 'the prison of great love.'"

"Which Villon wishes to escape?"

"Yes."

"Which I don't."

"Yes, I know."

"Par elle meurs les membres sains / Au fort je suis amant martir/ Du nombre des amoureux sains."

"Saints die for her? Do I get that right?"

"No. He's the martyred lover, one of the saints of love."

"He wishes to escape that? I don't get it."

"She doesn't love him back. *'Qui m'a este felonne et dure!'* She's feloniously hard on him."

"Feloniously hard? Are you sure?"

"You don't trust me? Literally, felonious and hard. Kinnell translates it 'criminally hard.'"

"I trust Kinnell. And is not all love 'criminally hard'?"

"Just ours, Sweetie. Just ours."

"And Villon's."

"And Villon's, yes," she said.

For their second anniversary, she gave him poems by Galway Kinnell himself: *The Book of Nightmares*.

"If one day it happens/ you find yourself with someone you love."

"It happened, Josie. Not in a café, not in Paris, but wherever I'm with you. How did the poet know?"

"I don't think he did."

"He calls it error to believe one day all this will be memory. He knew."

"What's important is we know," Josie said.

"You can believe you love and it may not be so, but you can't really love unless you believe you do," Jonah said.

"I didn't just believe, Jonah; I loved both. Josie hit me like a typhoon, but I couldn't drop Laura. There was too much to let her go."

"'The true is the name of whatever proves itself to be good,' William James."

"Yes. I was the supreme pragmatist."

"I'm sure Laura would agree."

"I think she'd insist truth is immutable."

"Yes, I think that's Laura," Jonah said.

"But I was happy and content. It seemed the practical application of my happiness to have both. Wouldn't James have agreed?"

"I think there's something not quite right in your reasoning," Jonah said.

"Robert wants to date me," Josie said one day in their third year together.

"Robert in Finance?"

"Yes, that Robert."

"Why would you date someone in Finance?!"

"What's this howling about his department? You want me to find an engineer?"

"I'd rather you found nobody."

"You have Laura. Why shouldn't I have Robert? We're only going on a date. Nothing will come of it."

"So you aren't dumping me?"

"Of course not. I love you."

"Then you're not going to tell him about me?"

"Not unless you tell Laura about me. You're not going to tell her, are you?"

"No."

"Then I won't tell Robert," she said.

And she didn't, he supposed. She dated Robert four months and Everett never asked about them. Her being with Robert limited when he could see her, but when he could, they were happy, playful, passionate. Nothing seemed different until she dropped Robert.

"You're not seeing him anymore?"

"He was falling in love with me. I couldn't allow that."

Something had happened in her seeing Robert, however. Changed what Josie wanted or what Josie needed or what Josie knew she could have.

"You must tell Laura about us," she said to Everett. "We can't go on like this."

"You don't love me."

"I do love you. That's what makes it hard, Everett. I know you love Laura, and I love the part of me that accepts that. But she has a right to know; she has a right to accept or not accept; she has a right to choose. It's wrong for us to go on without her knowing. You must tell her or we can't see each other anymore."

"Josie, Josie, Josie, Josie," he cried. "I don't want to lose you. I don't want to lose Laura. I can't tell her."

"You must, Everett. By Christmas. I know you're frightened, but I need this."

It was October. Sixty days seemed like a lot of time to Everett.

He'd stopped in a copse of stunted lodgepole where the river looped around an outcrop—a mile now, he estimated, from the trail junction. He lay by the water and didn't feel like moving. Before he'd collapsed, he'd climbed above the trail to shit behind a bush, watched dispassionately as dark blood oozed out of his stool and soaked into sand in the pit he'd dug.

It's not wise to shit blood in the woods. Wolves will eat your shit and come after you. He imagined a pack following him, their prints in a sandbar, him on his knees studying tracks to determine how fresh they were, listening to the hunting call in the evening to determine how close they might be. But there were no shit-eating wolves on the San Joaquin. The padres had tamed those beasts long ago, Christianized those canines, sent them away. "Go forth, Ye Wolves, in the name of Christ! Get now!"

The first time you shit blood, it scares you. You flush it away quick, tell yourself it was a ruptured hemorrhoid. Scratched yourself with toilet paper, or something. You wait for it to happen again; you hope it doesn't ever again, then it does. This time you don't flush. You almost pick it out of the toilet bowl to look at it, but don't need to. It's not bright red but dark, and blackish tendrils run out into the water as the stool settles. You sit on the tub and stare at the fouled bowl, and it stinks and you wonder why you don't reach over and flush it, but you don't. You sit and watch the water in the bowl turn reddish, and that's it. You forget you're staring at a toilet bowl half filled with dark water. A terrible sadness comes over you, a sadness for all the living and dead, and sadness too for this waste you cannot ignore, a sadness wet and oppressive, as if you were at the bottom of the reservoir that sends water down the pipe.

You flush, you stop being scared, you stop being sad. Nothing helps. You take your drugs and shit blood, and the will weakens.

"You are some piece of shit," he told his body, furious he was lying by the river and not hiking, furious all he was asking of his body was to get him one more time into Evolution Valley, frightened it wouldn't have the wherewithal. Given its druthers, his body would not move. Not a tattered coat upon a stick, Billy Yeats, but a crumpled pelt on rocks and roots, unless I get my ass up, "Unless/ Soul clap its hands and sing, and louder sing/ For every tatter in its mortal dress." Because it was far easier to clap than to get up, he clapped, in no particular rhythm.

He had no idea how long he clapped. Maybe all afternoon.

When he made an appointment, the first thing his doctor asked was whether he was in pain. "Yes, of course I'm in pain. I'm old" he said. — "Do you feel bad?" — "I feel fine." — "Appetite?" — "I eat a lot." After his examination, the physician said, "I don't know. There's nothing unusual in the rectal exam. I can feel some bumps in your lower back but that could be almost anything. I'm sending you out for some blood tests, and you'll have to get me a stool specimen. We'll check everything and hope we come up with a 'Good to go!'"

Everett left carrying a small stool specimen kit, an envelope he turned over and examined, amused at how innocuous it looked. He was tempted to tell passersby, "This is my stool specimen kit. Looks legal, doesn't it?"

Walking up University Avenue, he was stopped by the stench of a homeless man shitting in a doorway.

"Why don't you shit in a bag?" he yelled. "I have to shit in a bag. You could damn well shit in a bag too."

"Go away," the man muttered.

"I'll go away when you clean that up. No way you have to shit on the sidewalk. You can shit on a newspaper; you could shit in a bag."

The man just pulled up his pants and walked away.

"Do you need help down there?" someone was shouting. "Are you okay?"

Everett turned toward the caller. A young man was climbing down from the trail, watching him.

"Do you need help?"

"No. I was just clapping."

"I thought you were trying to get someone's attention. Do you want me to come down?"

"I'm all right." And to show that he was, Everett stood unsteadily. He tottered in his first step but was standing.

"You see? I'm okay."

"All right. I thought you were clapping to get someone's attention."

"I was just clapping."

The young man turned, climbed back to the trail, and went on.

"Clapping to get someone's attention? I should think not. Not some-one, but 'the Heavens above us.' Oh no, my fine young sprout, I don't clap to get attention. I clap to stay alive.

"And now that I have you standing, we're doing some walking, Buddy," he warned his body. "You have got to buck up; you have got to trek."

He spread his feet shoulder width and planted his stick, anchoring him-self to lift his pack. Wrestling it onto his shoulders and straightening, he rebalanced himself and climbed up from the river. Not allowing himself to rest when he made the trail, he walked, step after tiring step, like a man fastened to and dragging a weight—sheer willpower driving him forward.

"Consume my heart away; sick with desire/And fastened to a dying animal/It knows not what it is."

"Fastened," he chanted. Step. "Fastened to foot." Step. "Fastened to fiber." Step. "Fastened to fear." Step.

"Who are you to talk?" he demanded of his body. "Consume your heart away, fastened to a dying intellect?...YOU hate being fastened to ME?

"You have gall, I must say.

"I need you, but needing you is not being you. Got that, Sucka?

"It's ridiculous to think of you as ill and not to think of myself as ailing, but that's how it is. We have come to a time of ridiculousness. You may be done, but you're not taking me down with you. Not yet. Understand that?

"You, for sure, do not have a lot to bitch about. I don't think we ever passed a pub without having a pint, and that was fine. You loved it, I loved it. So don't come at me with that 'shackled to a dying intellect' crap. Okay, 'fastened,' you textual freak. The verb doesn't fucking change it.

"I can still think, you know, and if I didn't have to take the drugs to keep you going, I could still think clearly.

"You don't need the drugs, you say? Now isn't that some kind of fucking rich! There isn't a thing wrong with my brain except having to deal with my guts eating each other, and that's you, Buddy. Body. Flesh. There's no intellect to it, you bastard. This brain is no fool, I can damn well assure you.

"Oh pardon me, pardon me. You too are the brain. How could I forget your bringing blood? How could I forget your bringing oxygen? How could I forget your bringing pain? How can I forgive your fucking bringing pain? How can I forgive you bailing on me?

"We used to be an awesome team. We used to walk the walk. When we left aerospace, they gave us a basketball. 'To the kid who talks the talk and walks the walk.' They called us *kid* back then. They all signed it: the engineers, the production managers, the test managers. You were good back then. I had no complaints.

"Listen up, you fucker, we have got to find that walk again. Have to. If you think today is hard, just wait until tomorrow."

VI

The trail veered from the river, climbed a ridge studded with boulders and Jeffery pine, dropped to the river in a half-mile, crossed it to the south side on a footbridge, then paralleled the stream for a hundred yards before crossing the river on another footbridge to the north side and the junction for Evolution Valley. The flat was much used, vegetation obliterated where hikers had camped. The area within a hundred feet of the water had been posted with a NO CAMPING sign. Campers had moved back from the river, huge patches of bare dirt and trampled flora bleeding deep into the forest. The ground was picked clean. Even small twigs and pine cones had been gathered, burned, and lower branches snapped off trees. Already, three tents were set up for the night—two of them bright orange—erected inches past the boundary of the no-camping area. The third was off the trail, partially hidden behind a log.

Everett detested hikers with no sense of outdoor etiquette, those who'd raise a tent in an open space, shattering everyone's concept of wilderness as "man's work being substantially unnoticeable." Didn't people ever pay attention? Ever examine what they were doing? Didn't they care?

Riparian usage riled Everett. Camped at Davis Lake one night, Jonah called him the Elliot Ness of the John Muir Trail.

"You damn straight. Pick 'em up, cite 'em, send 'em off to the federal pen. And not Lompoc. I'd ship them to Pahrump, have them camp out in the yard in the summer heat. That should rehabilitate them."

"For riparian degradation, I think a court might find that cruel and unusual punishment," Jonah said.

"So they can wreck the creeks, camp where they want to, wash their dirty asses in our lakes and rivers? I don't think that's protected by the Constitution."

"People like to be by water. That's just the animal we are. 'We are haunted by waters.'"

"I can't believe you'd quote Maclean when we're talking assholes camping too close to streams."

"He was a fisherman, a multi-use guy. I don't think he'd complain as long as they stayed their hundred feet back. You aren't even satisfied with that, Everett. How far is that lake?" Jonah asked, pointing toward Davis Lake in the twilight. "A quarter-mile? We're camped in these rocks a quarter-mile from the water."

"It's no quarter-mile, and anybody could walk by the lake and not ever know we're here. That's what I aim for."

"And every time I hike with you, Everett, that's what you get. Your conscience should be clear."

Ah yes, Jonah, my conscience should be clear. You never liked the campsites I picked. I knew that, but I always fought to pick my spot, and now I'm punished with spots where I have to camp because I can't get to where I want anymore. A dozen times I've been through here and never stopped to camp. Not once. But that's not in it for me anymore.

Everett sat on his pack and wished he hadn't. Willpower was leaking out of him. He imagined his will flowing toward the river like snowmelt and leaching into the water, the San Joaquin diluting it. A hundred particles per liter, ten particles per liter, a hundredth of a particle per liter. At what dilution would his will be undetectable?

He saw Jonah one last time before he died. Heavily drugged, Jonah sat in his living room armchair, the chair in which he'd read for years, misshapen and tattered, fabric shiny along the armrests.

"Ellen can get rid of this thing when I'm gone," Jonah said.

"Who knows?"

"She will. She's always called this my dorm chair. She's been badgering me to throw it out for years."

Jonah's responses were slow. It seemed to take a long time for him to shape whatever he was thinking into words.

"I've read a lot of books in this chair," Jonah said.

"I know. You had it on Grant Street when we lived there as students."

"You don't have that place anymore, do you?"

"Long gone."

Jonah chuckled softly.

"Long gone. The Grant Street house long gone, but I still have the chair."

"Easier to keep the chair than the property. We sold the house when we moved to Sacramento."

Another long pause. Jonah straightened the left sleeve of his robe, placed his arm deliberately on the armrest, then turned as if he'd suddenly remembered Everett was there.

"You never liked Sacramento much, did you?" Jonah said.

"No."

"I never liked it either. Sometimes I was there two or three times a week, but I never moved."

"You were lucky to run a local office, not a state agency."

"It always surprised me you moved there."

"Laura had the job."

"Is she still there?"

"Yes."

"She was a fine woman, Everett. A fine woman."

"She still is, Jonah."

"And the other one?"

"Josie? I don't have contact with her anymore."

"After all that happened, you don't have contact?"

"That's life, Jonah."

"Isn't it," Jonah said. And after a time, "It doesn't bother me anymore to lose contact with someone. One day they're here, then they're gone. 'Lose contact' is a strange concept. It seems to lose contact with someone, you'd have to have found contact with them first, but we don't use that expression. You ever known anybody to talk about finding contact with someone?"

"I haven't."

"Nor have I. But that's silly, isn't it? I've become really silly, Everett. I don't know if it's the drugs or if it's just going through this end-of-life thing. 'You have to expect some cognitive loss,' I am told, 'but it shouldn't significantly impact daily functioning.' How's that for medical blather? It's not cognitive loss that's beating down my daily functioning; it's pancreatic cancer. And cancer doesn't care a whit for cognitive loss. It's a struggle to think clearly about the things I still want to think about clearly. Sometimes I get lost with a thought and follow it into a labyrinth. I get silly, just plain silly."

"It's okay. How much do you care?"

"A lot. I want to die with precision of mind like electricity that goes hot and straight through a wire until the moment a switch is thrown. No electrical loss, no cognitive loss. Like in the poem, I want a mind of winter. I want that clarity, Everett. I don't know if it's given to any man."

"Grab for it, Jonah. Stick with Stevens as best you can."

"As best as I'm allowed, Everett. I want to hang on to the very last moment, to the 'Nothing that is not there and the nothing that is.' I'm greedy. I want the nothingness too, Everett. It's the last thing I can have."

"I'm rooting for you, Jonah," Everett said, wondering what the hell that meant. Did he root for Jonah to die? For Jonah to have a good death? What made a good death, and what, in God's name, was there to root for?

They sat in silence until Jonah's hospice caregiver arrived.

"My Azrael cometh," Jonah said. "He will succor me now."

"Should I go?"

"I think so. Yes."

"I may not see you again."

"You may not, Everett," Jonah said. "We shall see."

A group of hikers crossed the bridge and dispersed into the camping area where Everett sat: five young people wearing bright shirts, convertible hiking pants with legs zippered off above the knees. They threw their packs down and started planning where to camp. Everett rose, wishing he were invisible, wishing he'd got his ass up before they arrived. He tilted his hat to cover his wound, but when he moved, everyone stared at his bloodied head. He tried to shoulder his pack nonchalantly, struggling to pull it to his shoulders quickly.

"What's wrong with you people?" he yelled. "Haven't you seen an old man before?"

"Your head's hurt," one of the young people said.

"I'm fine," Everett said, walking away as fast as he could.

There was no going on, but he had to get away from them. He passed the orange tents and the logs at the edge of the clearing, following a well-worn path through shrubs and grasses to the creek. The water flowed deep and swift, and the trail did not cross. Vegetation on the bank was tramped down where hikers had milled about. From his sightlines, he could see no white water but could hear the creek roaring as it dropped toward the river. Inching along the bank past unoccupied campsites where ground had been smoothed and fire rings built, he worked his way out of the riparian area and into the forest above. Within a hundred feet, the canyon wall tilted up sharply.

Talus spread laterally along the wall. The area behind it would do for him. Branches on a nearby lodgepole were high enough to hang food. Unpacking, he searched first for the leather pouch with his drugs, shaking out two Oxycontin, taking them one at a time and chasing each with a sip of water. Retying the pouch carefully, he placed it back in the pack, chose a granola bar, bit into it, sat on his pack.

He could hear the creek, riotous and constant. A shout went up from the campers below. Everett listened as the sound died away, vanishing into the roar of water. The granola bar in his hand was half eaten. He rewrapped it, slipped the bar into his pocket, rose to his feet. Moving a few rocks, taking care not to disturb the forest floor, he smoothed a spot for his sleeping bag. Laura always insisted on level ground for sleeping. It could be rocky, it could be wet, but it had to be level.

He rolled out his bag, hunted his counterbalance line, and crossed to the tree he'd chosen for hanging food. The line's hiss over the branch seemed loud, the stone's thud when it landed thunderous. He waited for these sounds to fade until all he heard again was the creek. The noise of the line and rock seemed to reveal his location, to what listener he knew not. Probably the campers below. It sounded as if more had arrived: someone laughed, a pot banged, a tent pole dropped. He felt confident they'd stay in the flat, away from his camp. They had Laura's syndrome, he suspected. All wanted a level bed. "Try the Marriott. Try the Hilton," he wanted to yell. Why some people backpacked had always been a mystery to him. He'd probably die without the answer.

Going for water, he retraced his steps to the creek and sat on the bank to fill his bottle. Made in China of biodegradable plastic—or so advertised—it was columnar, topped with a cap that allowed drinking from a spout. Everett felt the water go cold down his throat. So much of his body was lost to the drugs, so many sensations dulled. It was good the pain was tempered but good too to feel the cold water.

"You're not drinking from the creek, are you?" a piping voice behind him asked.

Everett breathed deeply but didn't answer or look around.

"Every stream here has giardia lamblia," the voice continued. "It can cause diarrhea, bloating, intestinal cramps."

The voice seemed to go shrill as it continued, shriller and faster.

"You have to filter or treat all water. You cannot drink from any lake, any stream. Even a stream from snow melt may carry the parasite."

Everett turned to look at the speaker: a young man, thin, medium height, dark haired, several days' growth of beard. His face was tanned, skin unblemished. His eyes gray, bright, concerned.

"You can't drink the water without treating it," he said again.

"What about piss?" Everett asked, still sitting. He did not have to stand for this. "Can I drink piss?"

"What are you asking?"

"Piss, urine, it's supposed to be sterile, isn't it? What if I find myself some coyote piss? Can I drink that without boiling it?"

"Urine is sterile. Why are you asking?"

"Piss is not sterile. That's why I'm asking. Because you don't know that."

"I was just trying to warn you."

"Why should you warn me? Do you think I care about giardia? Giardiasis is treatable. Even ignorance is treatable. Everything but death is treatable in today's world."

"Why are you angry?"

"I'm not angry. I'm just untreatable."

"I'm sorry," the young man said, turning and walking away. "Just don't drink the water, please."

Christ, it wasn't going to be easy. He'd planned for the miles, planned for the trail, but had not planned for the people. First the Julie woman grabbing him to dress his ear, now this kid quoting from the national park pamphlet on giardia. He'd expected solitude. He was going into the wilderness, wasn't he? Who'd think people would interfere? Well, going into a national park, any damned fool would. You'd more likely find solitude strolling up Powell Street than hiking the John Muir Trail.

Rising, he waited for his legs to steady themselves, then marched away from the creek to the talus shelf and his equipment. He felt safe there, above the fray, though when he sat on his pack and surveyed his surroundings, he realized he wasn't hidden at all. He was up the hill where almost no one would come, but exposed. Trees around him, but nothing to hide him at ground level. Anyone could wander by and step on him, but no way was he moving. No place to move to, no better sheltered spot he could see.

Dragging his pack toward him, he took out his food bag and chose dinner. After cutting thin slices of bread, then slivers of cheese, he laid his biodegradable bamboo knife down carefully.

"Don't biodegrade yourself yet, Buddy. I still need you."

"What would you rather be: driftwood or dirt?" a man asked a biodegradable bamboo knife. The knife didn't know. He'd never actually thought about it. He'd always known he was made of bamboo, grass not wood, but grass too could become driftwood. After all, this was America. Hell, this was California! You could recreate yourself as whatever or whomever you wanted. Why not driftwood? So the biodegradable bamboo knife said, "Sure, why not," and the man walked to the river to throw the knife in. When he got there, he thought, "If the knife can become driftwood, why can't I?" He jumped in with the knife in hand. They floated along, both excited about becoming driftwood until the river dropped in a thousand-foot waterfall. The man was smashed and dropped the biodegradable bamboo knife. The knife drifted into a logjam some miles below the waterfall. The man's body wound up in a backwater pool and began to rot when the river dried up in the summer. A bear smelled the carcass and ate him. A camper came up the river in late summer, gathering driftwood, and picked up the biodegradable bamboo knife. He burnt it in a campfire. So the knife went up in smoke and the man became bear shit. Things don't always turn out as planned.

"Don't worry," Everett told the knife, "I'll take care of you." He placed it back in the pack gently, as if it was sentient.

Dinner finished, he closed his food bag, knowing he had to get up and hang it, the nightly ritual. From where he sat, he looked across at the nearly bare south wall of Goddard Canyon. Sunlight had disappeared in the inner gorge and was edging up the rockface—a jagged shadowed line, tips of trees and the angled edge of canyon wall rising toward the crest. The creek roared through the darkening ravine behind him. Occasionally he heard campers, though they were surprisingly quiet. Maybe he'd misjudged them. Maybe they respected the space they'd come to, maybe they were too tired to be rowdy, or maybe the creek was drowning out every whoop and holler they let out.

Whoop and Holler indeed. Maybe they were drinking some good old Orphan Barrel hooch down there, enough to silence any crowd. The evening sunlight was the color of whiskey, and for a moment Everett conjured up the roasted-grain-and-oak taste of a finely aged spirit. The whiskey taste dissipated; evening color faded. A trace of sunlight remained, orphaned on the tips of peaks.

Getting up, he gathered food bags, hung them, peed, returned to the talus bench, and crawled into his sleeping bag. He was chilled suddenly, shivering, and lay still, wanting very much to rest, to really rest, to regain strength. If he could sleep ten hours and wake rested, he could do the wall tomorrow. He knew he could. Struggling to remember how many switchbacks there were, he pictured each zigzag where the trail swiveled back on itself. He'd probably stopped at every hairpin turn at one time or another—facing east to gaze up Goddard Canyon, facing west to look down the San Joaquin—but couldn't remember the number that lifted the trail out of the inner gorge. And that was only the start. After leaving the gorge, the trail swung in a long incline southwest toward the creek, then climbed along the stream into the basin above, past thunderous cascades as the creek dropped out of its hanging valley.

He loved this trail, recalling the many times he'd hiked it, especially that crazy afternoon with Randy after charging in fifteen miles from Florence Lake, Laura leaping down the trail to join them. "There'll be no Laura this time," he reminded himself. "You lost her." — "I never lost her. It's just some things are irretrievable." — "You abandoned her." — "I did not abandon her. I just couldn't keep her." — "So you lost her."

The commercial satellite subcontractor's Christmas party in Davis was a great success. Wine chosen by a sommelier, food prepared California style—salmon, crab cakes, prosciutto-stuffed artichokes, spiced cranberry almonds—all provided by the subcontractor, who had received an extension for thirty-two first- and second-stage rocket severance systems. Everett had been recruited as an independent contractor to develop and write the response to proposal. The party was hosted by the project lead and chief engineer, Brian Walsh, who was smitten with Laura.

"Where have you been hiding her?' he asked Everett.

"She's a legislative assistant. I wouldn't call that hiding."

"Well, that's nonsense. Why isn't she working for us?"

"She's after bigger fish, Brian."

"We'll see about that," he said, and spent the evening talking with Laura about music, community and civic action—while at Los Alamos Labs, Brian had sued the state of New Mexico to force it to provide school accommodation for his disabled child—organizational theory, and Alma Maria Mahler. Laura had been reading Alma's diaries and loving them. Brian's connection to Alma was much slighter: her last husband, Werfel, wrote the screenplay for *The Song of Bernardette,* which Brian had seen as an altar boy.

"Alma Mahler was his wife when he wrote that, no?"

"Yes," Laura said.

"So I have a connection to her."

"If you say so," Laura said, laughing.

"I was smitten with Jennifer Jones," Brian said.

"Being smitten seems a habit of yours," Everett thought.

"You were an altar boy? So was Everett," Laura said.

"Did the priest have you watch it too?" Brian asked Everett.

"Yes, like every good little Catholic boy," he said. "I was smitten with Vincent Price."

"He's pulling your chain, Brian. Go away, Everett," Laura said.

He wandered around the party sipping the good wine, sidling into groups of engineers; listening carelessly to discussions of explosive load, burn rate, explosive collision; watching Laura as she talked with Brian or as they moved around the room and met other partygoers. From everything Everett could tell, they were not talking explosive load. Brian would take Laura's elbow, lead her into another group, introduce her with some sort of joking remark—"You wouldn't believe: Everett's wife," probably—which always got a laugh. Whatever the joke, Laura would laugh and start talking in the new group. He relished watching her, delighted in her engaging everyone in precise, considered speech about what fascinated her. He wasn't surprised she found Alma Mahler seductive.

The party went on later than expected. Tule fog was settling into the valley, and no one seemed eager to go out in it. By the time Everett and Laura left, the fog had settled thick and ghostly, close to the ground, visibility approaching zero. They took the frontage road east toward Sacramento, crept onto the Yolo Causeway, drove in silence—faces close to the windshield, caution lights flashing—as they crossed, then exited immediately on West Capitol Avenue. Each breathed a sigh of relief.

"Can't believe we're out in this," Laura said. "We're such party animals. Once a year we go out, and we risk our lives."

"You were quite a hit."

"I had a marvelous time. I enjoyed being with you."

"I wasn't sure you remembered. Jeez God, Brian swept you up."

"I didn't forget whom I came with."

"I was scared you had."

"Why would I ever forget?" she said, placing her hand on his knee and squeezing.

They crossed the river on the Tower Bridge and continued home, the fog brightening in their headlights as they passed through.

When Everett came downstairs Sunday morning, he found a message on the answering machine from Tom, his boss. "Call Thompson. It's urgent."

He deleted the message, went out for coffee, and called Josie from a pay phone.

"Can you come?" she asked. "Something has happened."

"What?"

"I can't tell you on the phone. I don't want to tell you on the phone! Can you come?"

"I'll find a way."

"You must come. I need you."

"Is it bad?"

"Yes."

"Very bad?"

"Yes," she said.

Wide awake, Everett scanned the night sky. Trees grew in uneven clusters in crevices along the granite wall. Masses of stars hovered above him, ending abruptly at the canyon's rim as if the sky fit against Earth like a Lego block. Billions of stars, and billions beyond them, and yet room for dark space between, unfathomable dark space, and he found himself not seeing stars but looking into deep and endless darkness. Past the granite wall, past the Earth's edge, past the solar system, past the galaxy, past countless solar systems, countless galaxies, past the dimmest speck of light conceivable. The vastness into which he looked seemed strangely soothing. He dared not blink for fear it would dissolve.

A meteoroid streaked across his line of sight and dropped into a pine tree, falling through needles and branches. Everett's focus on the darkness broke. He again saw stars and treetops; he again could hear the creek. With such ease water drops and stars fall, but rising and moving were his problems. Getting up that wall tomorrow, especially if he lay awake all night. The ground under him was bumpy, but was that the problem? Hard to tell. Drugs took care of almost any discomfort. Maybe he could try tomorrow without pills, maybe pain would strengthen him. He tried to remember how long it'd been since he'd not worried about pain. It seemed forever. He knew he needed the drugs or the pain would stop him. Maybe he'd stay here an extra day, lie still, gain strength.

"Stop for a day and you'll never go on!" — "The wall tomorrow will take strength." — "You're not going to get stronger. You know that." —

"I could. I'd rest." — "You'll go; you'll do it. Stop the worry." — "I can't sleep." — "Count sheep. Count trees if you can't imagine sheep."

He counted the branches above him as best he could, not actually able to see each distinctly, but counting anyway. He reviewed scientific names for pine trees and subspecies. Jonah had known the Latin for each; hiking with him was like having a dendrologist in tow. Everett remembered *Pinus contorta var. Murrayana,* the Sierra lodgepole. Not as impressive as fir or cedar, but dominant. And *var. Latifolia,* the Rocky Mountain lodgepole, again not impressive but dominant from Colorado to the Yukon. The meek inherit the earth. The proof stands in *Pinus contorta.* Matthew got it wrong in his beatitude. Should have been talking trees, not hominids.

There was a subspecies Everett thought of, a *Pinus contorta* discovered in the Wallowa Mountains and named *var. Latifolia 'Chief Joseph,'* a dwarf tree with brilliant late-autumn foliage. Named for a man who'd fought stubbornly to live in the Wallowa Mountains but had been driven out, the shrub is difficult to propagate. Botany has its ironies. Joseph and the Nez Perce carried no dwarfed *var. Latifolia.* They crossed the Rockies through miles of lodgepole, then stopped in the Bear Paw Hills to hunt buffalo and never went on.

Joseph said, "From where the sun now stands, I will fight no more forever."

"You stop for a day, you're done!" — "The wounded and the old could go no farther." — "It's not the wounded who will stop you. It's your will." — "He wanted time to look for his children." — "If you stop tomorrow you will not go on."

Joseph said, "The earth and myself are of one mind. The measure of the land and the measure of our bodies are the same."

"I measure my bones against the granite, my body against the mountain, and the tally is equal for the earth and myself. But I'm not sure of my math, Joseph. Not sure of your premise either. The mountain and myself may not be of one mind. Tomorrow hard truth may unravel the reckoning."

VII

Enamel on grain. Crunch of husk, shell, nut. Floury paste on tongue. Sugary saliva. Chew, swallow. Take in more grain. Drink. Tongue clearing mouth. Dawn. Light spreading across sky. Gorge. Hydrate.

Everett sat facing the creek, his back to the canyon wall. It seemed to him the wall was waiting for him, studying his preparation with indifference. When he turned, he could make out the first switchbacks as narrow shadowy grooves scoring the lower mountain. A chickadee began to scold in a pine tree close by. Filling his water bottle, he rose and started.

The Nez Perce woke each morning to flight, knowing soldiers pursued them. Woke to hunger, fear, the swish of unshod horses. Gather the children, gather the wounded, leave the dying. They were led by Joseph. He started the people each morning, resolved disputes, arbitrated spats with tribal warriors. Move at first light. Onward. Forward.

The trail turned and he was on the second switchback, a long stone and rubble grade swinging toward the creek. He climbed steadily until he turned again, east toward Goddard Canyon. The sky was bright even though the sun was still below the horizon. How long would he have the trail to himself, he wondered, wishing he had the power to bid the sun stand still, not in the midst of heaven as had Joshua, but below the horizon. Bid the sun stand still, yes, but bid himself to walk. Sole to trail, sole from trail lifted, sole again. Sole, heel, sole. Heel, sole, heel.

August, 1877. W. T. Sherman, Commanding General, United States Army, was in Yellowstone Park, Geyser Basin, upper valley of the Firehole River. He left, assuring a group of fellow tourists they were in no danger from marauding Indians.

The Nez Perce followed the Madison River into Yellowstone, warriors, women, children, dogs, horses traveling together in one long plodding mass, stretching more than a mile. They were a grieving people, a people who had left a homeland forever behind them.

They captured the white people camped in Geyser Basin. The warriors—young, angry, bitter—wanted to kill them. The captives were given to Joseph to protect. He took their horses and supplies and sent them west, away from the Nez Perce. The Nez Perce fled on, racing toward what they hoped would be freedom in the White Mother's country, Canada.

He met his first hikers of the day, two young men. Bareheaded, shorts and t-shirts, light packs high on their shoulders, they shot past him, barely acknowledging his being there. Did they nod? He wasn't sure. One spoke and both laughed, short yaps like a squirrel barking, then were gone, switching down and back, down and back until they were out of sight.

"What was that?" — "What they said?" — "I couldn't understand it." — "Bet they're aiming for the 3:30 ferry." — "Ferry, my ass. They could be in Humphrey's Basin by tonight." — "That's what he said, 'We'll make Humphrey's before he gets to Evolution.'" — "Bullshit." — "They said it, I tell you." — "And that was funny?" — "To them, yes."

He wondered again how much longer he'd be able to hike alone. That seemed important. He'd be run over if he didn't move faster. Had to push himself harder.

Each step he watched his feet, determined to force them up and forward by concentrating hard. He imagined a line from nose to toe allowing him to lift a foot by tipping his head back. Brain to toe direct. Why route the message through an ailing body? Each switchback sloped up ten degrees as it went east, almost leveled as it ran back toward the creek and then, turning east, slanted up ten degrees again. He plodded along, bent forward, tilting his head with each step, cursing to himself, "Lift, you bastard. Lift!"

The Nez Perce forded the Yellowstone River at a crossing still called Nez Perce Ford, moved up Pelican Creek into the Lamar valley. They followed Miller

Creek into the Absarokas, the high barrier between the mountains and plains that stretched east toward the Dakotas, north toward Saskatchewan.

Once across the Absarokas, they killed every man, woman, and child they found: trapper, settler, tourist, traveler. No one could be left alive to reveal their location. It was not meanness, it was not vengeful. It was necessary. Theirs was not just flight, but a war to win. Sherman would have understood.

Hikers below on the trail were gaining on him, a group of six. He was surprised at how fast they hiked, seeming to zip back and forth across the switchbacks, nearly running compared to him. He pushed on, looking down occasionally on the tops of their heads, hats, and caps. Oh my God, one of them was wearing a wide brimmed sun hat. It couldn't be that Julie nurse; it couldn't be! He'd lost the bandage on his ear, and she'd surely grab him and go to bandaging again. He had to get off the trail, but there was no place in the narrow gorge. No getting away. No hiding.

The group soon passed. They were young and didn't ask about or question his being there. Why should they? He was just another hiker to Evolution Basin. "I've a right to be here," he told himself. "I can camp where I want as long as I'm back that hundred feet."

"Hard to get back a hundred feet here, Jonah. You know this canyon. It ain't the Yellowstone."

That summer they hiked up Lamar Valley, into the high country, the Absaroka crest. In the Hoodoo Basin, at last they were above the hillsides of stark ebonized trunks left standing after the great 1988 burn. For three days they'd hiked through grasses and flowers, each bloom and blade oblivious to what remained of the blackened forest.

"You know the old Nez Perce adage?" Everett joked. "'The grass smiles when the tree burns.'"

"No love lost between *Pinus contorta* and *Elymus trachycaulus*," Jonah added.

"What the hell is *Elymus trachycaulus*?"

"Wheatgrass, Everett, slender wheatgrass. Everyone knows that."

"The Nez Perce didn't know it. I don't know it."

"No love lost between lodgepole and wheatgrass. Is that better?"

"Much."

They'd been given a hiking permit to travel eight miles a day between designated backcountry camps, which turned out to be far too easy. Arriving early at each campsite every afternoon, they bitched about where they camped being dictated by park management.

"The Nez Perce camped where they pleased, I imagine," Jonah said.

"Not really. The army was after them. No small inconvenience."

"So they went down that canyon?"

"Six hundred, seven hundred men, women, and children, and more than a thousand horses."

"But we have to camp where the park ranger puts us."

"We're good *Injuns.* We stay in our little designated reservations. Times have changed, Jonah."

"Oh God, have they. I'd gladly settle for two miles today, Jonah. Just get me up this mountain. Two and out today, Jonah, and I'm done."

Clark's Fork and the Shoshone Rivers carve great canyons as they pour out of Yellowstone. The Nez Perce feinted to use the Shoshone descent. An army contingent moved to intercept them. They dropped instead down the Clark's Fork and out onto the plains, moving north now, safety ahead of them at last, a run for the border and their destination. O Canada. They hoped they could return to the old life there, but did not know if the old life could be had again.

Leaning forward like a draft horse, Everett clomped inside the retainer walls holding each switchback, eyes focused on drill marks where large stones had been split, calculating the footsteps these stones had known. Built by the Civilian Conservation Corps circa 1930, used eighty years now, open two hundred days—skip the winter months—thirty hikers per day, two feet for each hiker, roughly a million footsteps on each stone.

"On each stone I step the one millionth and one time. I do another step, another stone, and it too is the one millionth and one footstep. The foot moves. The stone is fixed."

A couple he had tried to stay ahead of caught up to him. The man was tall and had a full white, neatly trimmed beard, and friendly deep-blue eyes. The woman was small, and had long, dark hair. Quite attractive.

Her eyes too were blue and pleasant. They were probably well past middle age, apparently in great shape. They'd been hiking fast but didn't appear to be winded. Shedding their packs, they sat down, motioning for Everett to sit with them.

"It's a tough climb," the man said. "How far you going?"

"Just up," Everett said. "Up to the valley."

"It's not that far. Take a break."

Everett loosened his pack and slumped to a rock, took off his hat to wipe his brow. He was sweating profusely.

"That's a nasty bruise," the man said.

"I fell. Yesterday. No, the day before. It's all right."

"Are you alone?" the woman asked.

"My son's up ahead. And my grandson. And their friends. Lots of people. They'll be camped. They couldn't wait for me."

"Well, that's good," the man said. "I always liked hiking with our sons."

"They don't come with us anymore," the woman said.

"We burned them out when they were young," the man said. "We hiked everywhere. Brought them in here when they were only ten years old. So now they don't hike at all."

"I think they just don't go," the woman said. "They have busy lives."

"Maybe," the man said. "I still think we burned them out."

Everett said nothing. They seemed decent, but he wished they'd go. He was aching, needed medication, but didn't dare take anything while they were with him. He waited, he hurt, they lingered.

"Are you going soon?" he finally asked. They both stared at him.

"I'm sorry, I have to pee. I can't get off the trail, and I'd rather not do it in front of you."

"Sure, sure, sure," the man said. "Let's move, Ellie. This man needs his privacy."

"You're lucky your family is with you," the woman said. "It's always wonderful to be with family."

When they were out of sight, Everett rifled his pack for Fentanyl, slipped a capsule under his tongue. He had to be more careful, had to keep himself medicated. It was better to be weak than helpless, better to be slowed than stopped. There was no going on without the drugs. That was a fact.

The drug made him dizzy; he couldn't get to his feet. Shoving his pack off the trail, he crawled after it until he was lying propped against the hill-side, exposed to sunlight and passing hikers. Didn't matter. The wall was too steep to move farther. If he bit the dust here, he'd be the one millionth and one death on this trail. Of all those footsteps, how many were dead? How to calculate that, he wondered, then decided he didn't care. The pain and dizziness began to ease. He'd be fine. He was sure he'd be fine.

"Three years, and you never told me?" Jonah said.

"Why would I tell you? You'd have said, 'Great, Everett, you're cheating on Laura. That's really smart.'"

"I would not have said that. I'd have said, 'You damned fool. What do you think you're doing?'"

"And I'd have said, 'I can't help it. I love them both.'"

"After three years I believe you. You can't call three years a fling."

"It wasn't just an affair."

"You don't think Laura would call it that?"

"Of course she would. She'd have to."

"You haven't told her yet."

"No."

"You're going to stay with Josie and never tell Laura. How the hell is that going to work?"

"I don't know. I have to take care of Josie now. I have to be with her."

"Everett, when these things happen, when affairs become public, men stay with their wives, not their mistresses."

"Don't call her a mistress, Jonah."

"But she is. That's the relationship. You're crazy desperate now because of what happened to her, but she's your mistress."

"Are you going to loan me the fifteen hundred or not?"

"So you can put an alarm system in Josie's house without telling Laura? Borrowing money from me makes no sense, Everett. You have the money. Put the alarm in, but tell Laura."

"Josie was raped in her home, Jonah. She needs to feel safe. I don't know how to tell Laura. I can't spend fifteen hundred without her knowing."

"Then let her know."

"I don't know how, and I haven't time to figure it out now."

"I bet you don't. You have to tell her."

"I can't."

Jonah shook his head hard as if to clear it.

"I'll do it, Everett. Just don't tell Laura I did." And then, "You're making a mess of things, Everett. You're making a mess."

Sunlight dropped juniper needle shadows on his chest and backpack. How long had he been resting? Had he slept? Trees on the west wall threw shadows over the trail and over the switchback that ran east and disappeared around a cedar.

It was late afternoon, hot. Had it been hot when he'd stopped? Yes, he'd been sweating. The couple who stopped to talk with him had been sweating. Sierra hikers didn't sweat early morning. So it was later than he thought. Was he halfway? The couple, when Everett told them his destination was Evolution Valley, said he was close. What did that mean? A half mile, a thousand feet, ten thousand steps? How could people be so imprecise about distance? The couple was old enough to know better, but gauging distance was a gift few ever acquired. Not something he'd hold against them.

Whatever the distance, it was time to go. Determined not to be caught unmedicated, he took two Oxycontin. Threading his arms through the pack straps, he hoisted himself to a sitting position, let his feet slide onto the trail. That was the easy part. Standing not quite such a snap. He planted his walking stick, grasped it, lifted himself, stood, aligned his feet to move up the mountain, and stepped out. Evolution Valley was not far. That had been confirmed.

No hikers passed, going up or down. The gorge narrowed. Switchbacks grew shorter. He walked on the shadows of pine trees; by late afternoon the canyon wall covered the sun and he walked on the shadow of the wall. The trail was close to the creek now. He could hear the roar of crashing water, wished he could get to it, but hardly had strength for the trail, let alone scrambling over streambed boulders. Those days were gone. Those days didn't count anymore. What counted was each step on this trail this day, and he counted each step, lost count, counted again, forcing himself to keep walking.

He'd forgotten how steep the trail was. He'd underestimated how exhausted he'd be. On a boulder, he rested again, feet out in the trail.

"You know I didn't want to see you, Dad," Mariah said.

"Yes."

"But you came anyway."

"Because I'm your dad. I love you. I want a chance to tell my story."

"I don't want to hear it, Dad. What the fuck? After what you've done, you think I want to listen to you. Why'd you do it anyway, you bastard?"

"What could I do? Josie was raped, Mariah. I had to be with her."

"I'm not talking about the rape. I'm talking about the three years. Or was it four? How many times did you lie to me to be with her? How many times did you tell us you were off to work when you were off to fuck your sweetie?"

"Mariah, please."

"'Please,' Shit, Dad. How many times did you lie to me?"

"I tried not to."

"Oh, that's great. You tried not to. And how often did you lie to Mom? What was wrong with you? Whatever made you think you could treat us like that?"

"I'm sorry. I really tried not to."

"Tried not to what, Dad? Tried not to lie to us or tried not to be found out? What did you try harder not to do, Dad?"

"I tried hard not to hurt anyone. Everything happened so fast after what happened to Josie. I would hope you'd have compassion."

"I have compassion—for her. I have compassion for any woman raped. I love you, but I don't have compassion for you, Dad."

"It hasn't been easy for me."

"That's really pathetic. You rip our family apart and want me to feel sorry for you because your girlfriend got raped. *She* was raped, Dad. You weren't. I don't owe you sympathy for what happened to her."

"I'm sorry, Mariah."

"Yes, you're sorry. You're sad and foolish and weak. You broke things you should have known to cherish, Dad. You made your bed. Lie in it."

The breeze off the creek was moist and cool, evening rich with the scent of juniper, sage, trail dust. He could see the white froth of rapids where the creek flung itself down mountain. Spray hung momentarily against trees, then disappeared. He watched, he waited. He needed to go on.

A national park official came down the trail from Evolution Valley, traveling fast, carrying a large pack, wearing the old tried-and-true khaki uniform and campaign hat—the full regalia. He greeted Everett as he passed, walked a few steps, then came back. Everett noted the arrowhead patch on his sleeve: the snow-capped pyramidal peak, the sequoia, the bison. He could never look at the patch without wondering why a bison grazed under a sequoia. He understood symbolism as well as anyone, but it never seemed right to him.

"Are you camping in Evolution Valley tonight?" the official asked.

"Yes," Everett said.

The official slipped out of his pack, let it drop in the trail.

"Could I see your permit please?"

He was young, so very young, Everett thought, and clean, so very clean. He wore a park ranger's badge on his right breast, on his left a brass name tag with *LITVAK* incised into it in bold black letters.

"I'm with my son and his friends. They have the permit."

"If you hike on one permit, you should stay together."

"They wouldn't wait for me. You can see I'm slow."

"You're hurt too. What happened to your head?"

"I fell. It's getting better."

"I'm surprised no one waited with you. It's not that far."

"They were just here, hasn't been long. I'll get up there."

Litvak took a notebook from his uniform pocket and a short yellow lead pencil of the type found in small wooden boxes in libraries. Everett wondered if he'd pilfered it.

"What's the name on the permit?"

"Did you filch that pencil from a library?"

"The service issues these. A lead pencil always writes, you know."

"I know. Astronauts used lead pencils to write in space, both American and Russian. But lead tips flake away and particles drift in microgravity, and pencils are flammable, something the American program wanted to avoid. They spent money to develop a mechanical pen that would write in space. The American public came to believe they spent millions. You know how much they spent: $4,382.50. The American public never bothered to check the figures. Did they tell you that when they issued that pencil?"

"They did not."

"The American people are dumb as a pine tree, Litvak. They don't know shit, and they get excited about the shit they don't know."

"I appreciate your sharing that, but I need to go, and I need to know who has your permit. I need the name who drew it."

"Steckler," Everett said. "Abraham Steckler." Litvak wrote it down.

"And you are?"

"Jonah Steckler. Abraham is my son." Litvak wrote it down.

"And what is your destination?"

"Evolution Meadow. It's on the permit. Abraham has it."

Litvak wrote it down, closed his notebook, put the pad and pencil in his shirt pocket.

"You named your son Abraham?" he asked.

"I wanted him to be learned, and a prophet."

"And is he?"

"He's a wine merchant. But a good one, a successful one."

"Abraham Steckler—I'll have to look him up."

Litvak picked up and shouldered his pack.

"I should cite you for not having a permit but won't. I can, and will, check at the station that you obtained one. I'm glad you have people with you, Mr. Steckler. You don't look like you could make it much farther."

"I'm a tough old codger, Litvak. I was hiking up here when you were still in day care."

"That's really not that long ago," Litvak said, smiling. "Be careful." He turned and started down the trail.

"I was hiking up here when your daddy was still in graduate school!" Everett yelled after him.

"He went to medical school—he's a doctor!" Litvak yelled back.

He was walking fast, dropping away quickly. "Must be in great shape," Everett marveled. How far did he intend to go before he stopped for the night?

"Well, goddamn it, I was hiking up here when your granddaddy got on the goddamned boat in Lithuania!"

"Lithuania" echoed up the narrow defile, but he wasn't sure Litvak heard.

Everett shuffled along. Commands to his feet took time to get there, and every muscle in calf and thigh seemed to wait for instructions before it flexed or extended. It wasn't as if he had a cellular rebellion on his hands, just that his cells didn't know what to do, as if his muscle memory had faded to that of a ten- or eleven-month-old whose memory didn't include walking.

Perhaps the secret was to walk without mind, move without thought. Forget the Zen masters and mindfulness, forget the deep breaths and exhalations, forget the present moment. March mindlessly. Let the bits of rock in the trail and the root scarred by footsteps distract you.

But there was no marching mindlessly for Everett. To keep going he counted steps in sets of eight, leaning forward, watching each foot move, then a set of ten, then twelve. He couldn't make fourteen. "You can't cut the mustard, you can still lick the jar. You can't walk the trail, you can still lick the stones." He imagined himself on hands and knees, licking stones, crawling on.

He made it to the drift fence below Evolution Meadow and opened the pole gate. The end post was propped in a rock pile, not anchored. It gave under his weight when he leaned against it. He thought of leaving the gate open; he had thought often of ripping out all drift fences to allow horses to run free. "Get the horses out of the high country. Protect the trails. Protect the land."

Jonah argued drovers would obviously bear the brunt of such activism, having to recover the horses—not the companies who sold the guided trips, who bought and owned the stables and mules and horses, nor the consumers who paid to ride instead of hiking. But was there an ethic for high-country activism? Must the activist consider drover impact? Did not the ends justify the means?

They'd never worked that out, never worked out the right to ride versus the right to hike, to leave only footprints or hoof prints, to leave only human shit or horseshit. Nothing had been resolved in their lifetimes of hiking. Standing with hand on post, bone-tired but unable to lean against it, Everett felt overwhelmed by what remained unsettled.

"There are tons of data on land and water use, scant data on horseshit. It is criminally understudied, Jonah. Criminally. You should have made horseshit your life's work. All your labor-management studies would have meant more if you'd studied the horseshit. We obsessed about war, history, human decay. We should have had an eye for horseshit, Jonah. We should have obsessed the horseshit."

He closed the gate and went on, ever slower, walking in sets of eight steps, pausing, then sets of six. Twilight was fading. Thirsty, he had to get to water. The trail turned toward the creek, to a ford where hikers were expected to cross and camp on the other side, but Everett wouldn't wade it tonight. He'd bed down this side, somewhere hidden in the trees and bushes.

"Let Litvak find me. He can write me up in his notebook."

Shaking arms out of backpack straps, he sat heavily on the stream bank. He lifted water in palms, drank, splashed more on his face, then was cold, shivering as his skin dried. Digging for the down jacket in his pack, he slipped into it and zippered up, but still shivered. He needed to get in his sleeping bag, but also needed more water. Hands shaking, he struggled to fill his bottle and cap it.

Dragging his pack, he hobbled away from the creek. The trees were not back a hundred feet. So what? He wasn't camping. He was just lying down, resting, at the end of his strength. The ground was dry; he could bed down.

He fumbled his pad and sleeping bag out, but didn't stop shaking when he'd slipped inside. There was a coldness flooding him he couldn't check, a coldness approaching paroxysm. Like the pain, it came at him from inside. It bored into his brain, not his skin. He grabbed his medication, slipped a capsule under his tongue, then lay down and waited. His pack was open beside him. There'd be no hanging food in counterbalance tonight.

"If the bear comes, he can eat me."

The drug began to temper the cold. He could imagine the warmth inside the belly of a bear.

VIII

"You don't have to talk, Josie. I'd understand."

"You'd understand waking with someone choking you? Having a knife stuck up your nose? You'd understand being told he'd cut Teddy's throat? 'Wake her, Bitch. I'll slit her gullet.'

"I prayed for Teddy. I prayed for her bedroom door to be shut. 'Oh God, please God,' I prayed. I let him do what he wanted. I did what he wanted."

"You had no choice."

"I thought I'd have to fight him. He'd kill us anyway. I should have fought him. I couldn't. Even when he hit me, I didn't hit back. When he slapped me across the face and said, 'I'm going to fuck you stupid,' I still didn't hit back."

She stopped, and Everett wanted her not to go on.

"I can't believe what I did," she said.

"It's not your fault."

Josie stared at him, dumbfounded.

"He tore open my pajamas, ripped the bottoms off, told me to spread my legs. I said, 'Please.' I can't believe I fucking begged him. One minute I'm begging God, and seconds later I'm begging this slimeball.

"I was scared crazy. I'd have done anything to have him leave. And when he finished, I couldn't help myself. I cried. I couldn't hold back the tears. I cried in front of that asshole."

"It's okay," Everett said.

"What's okay?"

"It's okay that you cried."

"It wasn't, Everett. Don't you understand? Nothing's okay. Nothing was. Nothing is."

IX

Warm in his sleeping bag, even sweating a little, Everett wakes in the dark, the Big Dipper overhead. He follows the end stars to find Ursa Major, needing time to locate the dimmer head and nose. Ursa Major looked like an insect to Everett, though Jonah insisted anyone could make out the bear easily.

"If you want to call that constellation Ursa, you better bring your own bear."

"It was Ursa as early as Ptolemy," Jonah said.

"Ptolemy and your ancestors laid around at night, hovering around campfires, scared shitless a bear might grab them. They saw bears everywhere, even in misshapen stars. If they'd been naming constellations in Africa, they'd have called it Anteater. That's what it looks like—a goddamn anteater. Long snout, long tongue: Vermilingua Major."

"The tail used to be short, like a bear's."

"Before the stars were fixed, I assume."

"After. Zeus stretched the tail when he moved the bear to align the Dipper due north. Common knowledge among ancient Greek sailors."

"He must have stretched the nose and legs too."

"He may have," Jonah said. "A godly tug can cause distortion."

Everett could hear something scratching inside his pack. Maybe Zeus had shrunk a bear and slipped it in there. When he moved the pack, the noise ceased. He waited for a few minutes and could hear something scratching again, a scratching that seemed amplified in the darkness. The crash of Evolution Creek was distant and muffled—the commotion in the pack loud and immediate. He ran his fingers along it to the side pocket, where he kept matches and candles. The noise stopped at once.

He found the candles and lit one. The area under the trees brightened like a stage. He'd bedded down on what in the spring had been swamp. Semicircles of pine needles were racked where they'd washed to the edge of the pool. Dried hair grass framed his sleeping bag.

Whatever was in the pack was quiet, perfectly quiet, as if listening to him. He set the candle in sand and turned the pack sideways across his belly, not wanting anything leaping out by his face. Protecting his medications, he removed them from an outside pocket and slipped them in his sleeping bag, then folded back the pack's top and waited. Nothing fled, nothing darted out. What had he expected? He rotated the pack cautiously until he could see inside.

His paper food bag was on top. It came out easily, but all food—granola, cheese, bread, nuts, dried fruit, chocolate—fell through the bottom. Something had chewed holes in it—neat, round, overlapping holes—and the bag had ripped completely as he pulled on it. When he looked into the bay, a field mouse stared back at him, its beady eyes shining, tiny nose twitching.

"Some bear you are," Everett grumbled. The mouse dived and disappeared under granola bars.

The bottom of the pack was littered with chewed paper, wrappers, nuts, granola, debris of every kind from his food cache. "Get out of there, you little bastard!" Everett scolded, reaching into the wreckage to shoo out the mouse. Not one but four mice leapt from the refuse, scurried across his arm, and ran. Ignoring the damaged food, he retrieved his packet of reading material.

For years Everett carried books on backpacking trips: poetry, novels, histories, volumes calibrated per length of trip. As he aged and hiking became more challenging, he began to gauge every ounce he carried, began to photocopy poems he wanted to read for the first time, poems he wanted to read again, poems he wanted to memorize, essays, sections of histories, parts of novels, short stories. He'd staple these together and carry only that booklet. Half those pages had been shredded by the mice—segments of Auden, Yeats, Whitman—and mixed with granola and nuts. A chewed label from beef jerky nestled with four lines of Shakespearean sonnet—"an ever-fixed mark, that looks on tempests and is never shaken" fallen to a mouse tooth. Shaking out gnawed bits of food, he flipped through the pages.

"They've eaten my Auden, Jonah. Look at that. Every verse. Half my Yeats, half my Whitman. They didn't touch Stevens. What is there with Wallace they found so unappetizing? Is it 'the junipers shagged with ice'? A bit too much to bite into there, huh?"

Spreading the booklet on his lap, smoothing pages, he checked for damage, thumbed to the next and the next, then stopped at a favorite Stevens poem. The candlelight was bright enough to read by. He ran his finger along each line as he read it to himself: "She sang beyond the genius of the sea," finger moving, following the singer, the sea, the lines of the poem. He paused and lifted his head as if to listen for the song before the finger moved again; another verse, longer pauses, then whole stanzas traced silently in the dim light, flame guttering in night breezes he did not feel, shadows he did not notice flickering on boughs above his head as he read on, until he spoke aloud fragments of lines he knew by heart. "The maker's rage to order words of the sea /... In ghostlier demarcations, keener sounds."

He sat with hands folded across the page, unmoving, listening.

Those first nights, Josie would sit in her reading chair long after Everett lay down, not even pretending to read, elbow on the chair's arm, chin in hand, staring at him. In time she'd rise and come to bed, and he'd open his arms to her. Sometimes she'd lay her head on his shoulder and fold her hands on his chest, and he'd hold her as she drifted to sleep. When he felt her relax, he'd listen to and treasure her every sleeping breath. Steady and safe she breathed, and he listened until he too fell asleep. Sometimes she lay apart in the bed, away from him, very still, and he too lay very still.

Some nights he woke to find her out of bed, standing by the window, peering out into the night. Although she knew he was awake, often she said nothing, then would get back in bed to lie next to him, or to lie apart from him. When she chose to lie apart, she'd reach over and touch him gently to let him know, that wherever she'd been as she stared into the darkness, she was in the bed again, hoping to sleep.

Some nights she'd speak without turning from the window, knowing he was awake.

"I'm so angry," she said one night. "I'm so damned angry I sometimes don't know how to function."

"It's all right, Josie. You should be angry with him."

"It's not just him I'm angry with. I'm angry he's out there, angry he gets to walk around, to go out in the day and walk along the streets. I'm angry he can do that, and nobody knows who he is. I'm pissed no one knows what he is.

"I'm angry nothing happens to him. I'm angry no accident strikes him down. Accidents are supposed to happen, aren't they?"

"The police are trying to find him."

"And I'm angry they'll never find him. They won't, you know. He's too damned smart, too damned clever. Good God, he used my own kitchen knife, but they haven't a single fingerprint for him."

"That's not their fault."

"Then whose fault is it? Why is he still out there?"

"Josie, stop, please."

"And I'm angry with you. I'm angry you listen to me. I'm angry you have no answers. I'm angry you're here. What are you doing here anyway?"

"I love you. I'm here to help you feel safe."

"And I'm angry that I feel safe when you're here. I should feel safe by myself. That's what I need. I'm angry I don't feel safe by myself."

"Do you want me to go?"

"No," she said. "But I'm angry too that I don't want you to go."

One night he got out of bed, found a candle in the bathroom, lit it. She turned and watched him carry it into the bedroom and set it on the dresser before he got back in bed. She stared at the candle for a moment, then walked across the room and blew it out. She crossed back to the window and looked out again.

"It's not the dark I'm afraid of, Everett," she said.

"Sometimes," she said on another night, "I think he's not all bad. He didn't kill me; he didn't kill Teddy. He could have killed both of us."

“You don’t owe him that kindness, Josie. He raped you. You should hate him.”

“I should hate him?”

“You don’t have to hold anything back.”

“Sometimes I dream of him being castrated. He’s tied to a stake. He’s still wearing the hood, still wearing the gloves, the blue t-shirt, but he’s naked from the waist down. Everything gets cut off, and he screams, and I enjoy watching it. Is that hate enough? Am I holding anything back?”

“I should have fought him. If I’d screamed and yelled and hit back and smashed him—there are a hundred things in here I could have hit him with—if I’d somehow detained him until police came, he wouldn’t be out there anymore.”

“You did what you did, Josie. You did the right thing.”

“How do you even know what the right thing is?” Not turning to Everett for an answer, she spoke out the window into darkness. “He’ll beat another woman because of me, he’ll rape another woman because of me; someday he may kill a woman because I was too scared to fight him.”

“You are not responsible for what he does, Josie.”

“So says you. How could you ever know what I’m responsible for? How could you ever know how much I hate myself?”

Weeks passed. Nights Josie watched at the window became rare. Everett looked for what he chose to believe were signs of recovery: a sudden smile, an unexpected laugh, a burst of mindless play with Teddy. When they made love again, when she came to him openly, he felt he held a treasure that had been damaged but not destroyed. But Josie was a scarred woman. Memories of her rape remained fresh and haunting, rising often to taunt her. The treasure Everett held that first time, and the second, fifth, and fiftieth fractured easily and needed time to repair itself. His greatest fear: she’d never fully mend and he’d lose her forever.

X

Sunlight high in the morning sky woke Everett, pouring through the boughs above his nest in the trees. He shoved his backpack off his sleeping bag.

Waking included moving carefully, waiting for what pain might come at him. His first thought was whether he'd taken pills the night before. He couldn't remember, reasoned he must have or wouldn't be pain free now. Pain free, "Aye, there's the rub." No healthy brain wakes to wonder if it's pain free. No healthy brain thinks of pain free until its body is wounded or torn, and what is wounded or torn repeats its cry of pain weekly, daily, hourly, continually.

"Pain management is a medical approach to the prevention, diagnosis, and treatment of pain. Pain management requires identifying the precise source of the pain and isolating the optimal treatment."

There's no limit to professional gibberish. Clinicians love to talk pain because it's not the illness they have to talk about, not the killer prowling the body, but the keening cells left in the killer's wake, the threatened tissue and organs approaching panic mode. The panic mode must be managed even as the assassin approaches. When the first drugs mask the pain, the mind lets go its caution, believes earnestly, if briefly, there is a way out. But the optimal treatment is no panacea; the optimal outcome remains a dead end.

"In six or eight weeks, we may need to go to a pump; the Oxycontin and Fentanyl should hold you for now. Use the Fentanyl sublingually for breakthrough pain; use the Oxycontin for sustained relief."

All cool, all calmly laid out, dominoes lined up. "Careful! Don't tip that tile!" How precisely everything is covered: number of milligrams per milliliter; number of micrograms per hour. Number of days drug required: an estimate.

"Just give me the damned medication. I know how to pop pills."

Gathering candles and matches dropped the night before, he tossed them in his pack, then rolled up his sleeping bag—meds still inside, poems and essays still inside, everything he'd stored in the bag before he discovered mice—and stuffed it in the top. He tied the pack securely, hunted for his shoes and trusted walking stick. Making his way out of the trees, he followed the trail to the ford.

Evolution Creek gleamed in morning sunlight, a series of green pools and clear shallows. A breeze ruffled the surface, driving sun-sparkling riffles upstream, masking the current. The water appeared thigh deep, maybe less; the ford's gravelly bottom seemed to invite wading.

A log lay near the trail where it approached the creek, extending out into the water. Everett sat to take shoes and socks off, intending to put the shoes back on and wade.

Four hikers came up the trail. Two men, two women, two with quality Osprey backpacks—hard to miss the brand names. They talked excitedly among themselves. "So this is where we cross?" — "Looks like it." — "You taking off your shoes?" — "Don't know." — "It's going to be cold." — "Yes it is." —"I think I'll keep my shoes on." — "Okay." — "Doesn't look that deep." — "Not really." — "Looks easy." — "Yup."

After a while they turned to watch Everett, who sat barefoot on the log watching them.

"Are you wading barefoot?" one of the young men asked. Everett said nothing.

"Is it best barefoot or wearing shoes?"

"Ed Abbey said the proper way to cross a stream was to take off your shoes and socks, put your socks in your pocket, put your shoes back on, wade across, take off your shoes and dump the water out, put your socks back on, put your shoes back on, and keep hiking."

"That's the best way?"

"That's what Ed Abbey said."

"Sounds right—exactly the way he said it."

"He also said, 'growth for the sake of growth is the ideology of the cancer cell.'"

"That's interesting."

"Most people wouldn't think of a cancer cell having an ideology. Most people don't get that far in their thinking."

"I suppose not," the young man replied, edging away.

The four crossed as Everett had told them to, taking off shoes and socks, putting socks in a backpack pocket, putting shoes back on, wading across with much hooting about the cold water, taking off shoes again, dumping water out, sitting on their packs to put socks and shoes back on.

"Abbey would be so damned proud of me," Everett thought.

"Abbey never said dog shit about wading a creek," Jonah said.

"How do you know? Could be something he said but never wrote down."

"And you were there when he said it?"

"Steve Ferris was, and I know because Brooks Trotmore knew Steve Ferris in New Mexico, and one night when Brooks and I were out drinking, he told me Steve Ferris heard Ed Abbey say that. He especially remembered Abbey cautioning to pour water out of the boot. Brooks said Steve Ferris said Abbey was emphatic about it."

"Abbey certainly wouldn't put dry socks in a boot full of water," Jonah acceded. "Scotch and water, yes; socks and water, no. That's Abbey."

Shoes on, the hikers disappeared up the trail. Everett slipped bare feet into shoes, thought of medicating himself, but decided he'd never get going if he did.

He waded into the ford, cold water sweeping around ankles and calves. There was a surprising current, persistent, a downstream nudge against both legs. He shuffled forward, planting the walking stick, stepping, planting the stick again, stepping again. His calves began to tingle; sharp prickles ran up his thighs like sewing needles stitching seams in his skin. It was an interesting sensation. He found it almost pleasurable compared to the pain that had wracked his body for months. This was bearable, a surface twinge. Stick down, two steps; stick down, two steps more. He watched his shins emerge from the water as he rose out of the ford, then his ankles, then the tops of his shoes. He was across.

Leaving the trail, he followed the creek downstream to where it spread over exposed granite and spilled out of the meadow. Sliding like liquid glass, it picked up speed, forming runnels in its first drop, white water in its second, rapids in its third; then it tossed itself into a chasm where years of flow had formed a bowl.

In an open space back from the creek, Everett plopped down on dry rock, warm from morning sunlight. Removing and emptying wet shoes, he sat with feet flattened against the slab but couldn't rest comfortably. His guts felt like barbed wire wringing itself around his lower spine.

"You can't stop, can you, you fucking replicating bastards! Why don't you learn from the goddamned granite? Let the skin flake, compress the core, sustain. A glacier cuts you a clean shave, you accept, you sustain. Where's the mystery, assholes?"

He pounded his midriff with the heels of his hands. There ought to be a way to knock the pain out, to beat sense into the cells eating his insides. He hated their mindlessness, hated his body having lost control of them, hated that cells he considered his to command would act without his bidding and to his detriment. He rolled across the rock to find his medication. Popping a Fentanyl, he waited, fighting nausea.

"Hell, Jonah, there's a lot more to life than pain management. There's nausea management, breath management, fear management, despair management. It's all out here for the taking."

"I can't believe this, Everett," Laura said.

"I'm sorry."

"How could you let this go on, for four years?"

"Three."

"I don't care. It's fiendish."

"I wanted to tell you. I tried to tell you, but after a while I couldn't. A year went by, then two. It made no sense, but I couldn't, Laura. It was too hard."

"Too hard? For you too hard? And it never occurred to you how hard it would be for me?"

"I thought of you, Laura. I thought of you all the time."

"Bullshit, Everett. If you'd thought of me, you'd have told me. I could have heard this the first month, maybe even the first six, but not after four years. I cannot countenance a sensitivity that calloused. I cannot."

"I'm sorry."

"You bastard. I've lived with you twenty years and never knew you were a bastard."

"I deserve that. I know how you feel."

"You deserve? You know how I feel?

"Forgive me."

"I will not, Everett. I'm not good at hating, but I'll hate you as best I can."

Sunlight covered Everett like a bedsheet. Occasionally a breeze lifted the sheet, and the air ran fast and cold from bare feet to face, then died and dropped the sun's warmth over him again. He moved closer to the creek, lay flat against the rock, head inches from the water. He could hear the creek sliding past, a blade of water stropped against a whetstone of rock. Did either water or rock have a concept of the other? Did either know they were siblings, destined to be together? Did granite remember its past as liquid, the giddiness of molecules moving randomly, safe in the womb of Earth, allowed to shape itself into crystals? Did water remember the earth's molten core or the stars it was flung from? Out of planetary rock dehydrated or stellar vastness dropped to flatten itself into Earth's every fissure and interstice, inveigling itself into plant and animal, trickster changing forms to fit any circumstance. Yesterday vapor; today water; tomorrow snow, ice. Inevitably, water again. Surely the embryonic planet and stellar mother were lost to memory.

In Everett's cells, he too carried memories: molecules accreted from solar dust, particles polished by glacier and rock. He squeezed eyes shut to conjure a planet forming, evolving, enduring—all he knew of permanence. In time, he opened his eyes and squinted at bright sun and sky. There was no compassion in consciousness.

Twisting away from the creek, he scooted across to his backpack. Upending it, he shook dried vegetables and fruit, jerky, energy bars, bread, cheese, and granola onto the rock with the meds, papers, candles, and matches. Most of the food packets had been chewed open, half the energy bar wrappings chewed away but the bars themselves not touched. His reading papers were only partially consumed.

"A candy wrapper is equal to a couplet. Understand that, poets. What matters is the fiber, not the aesthetic."

He sorted food into bags less damaged until only granola remained scattered on the rock. Winnowing it, he blew out the shreds of paper the mice had left, turning the cereal, blowing again—at last satisfied it was clean. He ate a few handfuls, scooped it up and dropped it on a bandana, securing it by tying the four corners. Repacking, he stuffed the sleeping bag in first, then food and papers. Candles and matches went back into a side pocket, meds as before into the front pocket. Tying the sleeping pad on top, he put on shoes and socks and shouldered the pack.

"We better get our butts to Colby Meadow, Fellows. You never know when Litvak might come storming through here."

He made his way to the ford, heading upstream. The trail circled through trees that grew along the meadow. The creek wound wide and green through grassy swales. Lodgepole had invaded the upper end, sending out seedlings where soil drained enough for them to survive. The Hermit, pyramidal and massive, loomed like a Buddha above the vista. Plunging into woods, the trail left the creek, then curved back again, a mother returning to check on her child.

"If you're not going to be here, you have to tell the children," Laura said.

"Mariah isn't even here. I'd have to go to Santa Barbara to tell her."

"Then go to Santa Barbara. You have to tell her."

"Then you tell Conrad."

"I won't. You tell him."

"That's not fair. You're part of this."

"You dare speak to me of fairness? Fuck the piece of work you've become, Everett!"

"It's not a question of whether I can ever trust you again," Laura said. "When someone for that long gives his time, his thoughts, his plans, his affection, and yes, his love, to someone else at the same time he cohabits with someone who believes he is giving her his time, his thoughts, his plans, his affection, and his love, and when he continues that without feeling compelled to tell her of the hoax being played, he's not just a hypocrite; he is cruel, he's unkind. How could you be unkind, Everett?"

"I never intended to be."

"Two weeks ago I couldn't have imagined life without you, couldn't have imagined Laura without Everett, the two of us a constant, a marriage I wanted and treasured, a life that included another person I loved, a life that embodied respect and trust, each valued highly. Two weeks ago that was my life, and now, Everett, I cannot imagine life with you. You're not that Everett anymore."

"I'm still Everett."

"You're not the Everett I loved. And I don't want the Everett you've become."

Parallel to the meadow, the trail followed the contour of the valley, nearly flat. Everett was pleased at how effortlessly he could walk.

"Nothing wrong with a smooth path," he thought. "'Let me loaf and invite my step.'"

"I will go to the bank of the wood and become undisguised and naked," Whitman announced.

Behold, the poet springs forth and makes his way in the wilderness!

"Let's walk first, Walt. We can do the undisguised and naked later. The 'bank of the wood' isn't going anywhere."

Ahead on the trail, young, bearded, brimmed hat cocked at an angle, work shirt open at the throat, "afoot and light-hearted," stepping lively and exaggeratedly, Whitman outdistanced Everett, then returned to gesture and declaim. "Shall I postpone my acceptation and realization and scream at my eyes,/ That they turn from gazing after and down the road?"

"Your acceptation is fine here, Walt."

"Still here I carry my old delicious burdens."

"We all do, Walt. Get on now.

"And where were you yesterday while I was climbing that rude, silent, all-too-comprehensible wall? There wasn't much of the 'earth never tires' in that. I was damn well discouraged. You show up, Walt, when the path is gentle, the way forward painless. Straight is the gate and narrow the path to Colby. Don't expect a lot of your 'divine things well envelop'd' along the way."

The trail angled up an outcrop that formed a barrier between Evolution and McClure, the meadow upstream. Hiking uphill, Everett reverted to his old plodding, leading with his walking stick, leaning forward, bringing one foot forward, then the other, then the stick again. When a pack train met him at the apex of the outcrop, he scrambled off the trail to the lower side, sliding farther downhill than he wished, braking himself with his stick.

Three riders passed silently, drover in front, three pack mules heavily ladened, followed by four more riders and another drover bringing up the rear. The last rider was huge, ass filling the saddle from horn to cantle, buttocks drooping over each side, thighs sagging against the saddle skirts like boat fenders. The chin strap of an equestrian helmet, cinched tight under double chins, divided them like brain lobes. Hands resting on the saddle horn, his bare arms jiggled.

His horse didn't seem to mind his weight and followed the horse in front, head down in line, requiring no rein. The rider looked left and right, and made eye contact with Everett.

"You're not that far," he said. "You're almost there."

"How the fuck do you know?" Everett shouted.

"McClure Meadow is just ahead."

"You don't know I'm going to McClure!" Everett yelled. "You don't have the slightest idea where I'm going."

"Don't scare the horses," the drover said.

"You couldn't scare his nag with a fucking atom bomb."

"Calm down, calm down," the drover said. "Keep moving, keep moving," he told the fat man, who was turning in his saddle to look back at Everett.

"He started it. Here I am trying to walk, and he's parked up there on his fat ass with the gall to tell me where I'm going."

"Go on, go on," the drover said, riding past Everett. "Thanks for yielding the right-of-way, Partner," he added.

Everett watched the drover's back recede, blue workman's shirt, dark-brown vest, colors that melted into forest as the pack train descended.

Everett was shaken and shamed, shamed that anyone riding in a pack train would dare speak to him, especially someone fat as a bratwurst. And shaken, he'd yelled at the rider. What kind of idiocy was that? Litvak had been bad enough. Now he'd alerted the whole damned national park staff and pack train drovers that a madman was on the loose in Evolution Basin. How soon would they be coming for him?

"Just get your ass to Colby and off the main trail. Cross the damn creek and you'll be fine."

Poling with the walking stick, he scrambled back to the trail, and was quickly over the outcrop. He hustled up the creek, almost loping, but could not sustain the pace. He slowed, paused, took meds. Not allowing himself to sit down, he leaned to rest against first one tree, then another, waiting for some miracle of revitalization he had little hope would come. Standing wasn't that tiring—his legs were fine—but his muscles seemed unresponsive to commands. Connections lost, it was hard to talk sense to them.

"You're not going to stop me, understand. I know you're aching, but we're going on."

And he did go on, trudging step after step.

To Everett's relief no park employee was at the ranger's cabin when he passed McClure Meadow. Door shut, the cabin was apparently uninhabited. Four hikers were having lunch on the stoop, gear strewn about like jackets in a schoolyard. Three other hikers were eating by the creek, shoes off, feet in the water. Everett hurried past. He felt exposed, unable to get across as fast as he wished, glancing behind him to check the trail, half expecting the drover or the fat rider or Litvak to materialize.

"There he is! " the fat rider shouted. "The horse shouter."

"That's Steckler. I know him. Did you shout the horse, Steckler? Did you?" Litvak yelled from the edge of the woods.

"I did!" Everett yelled back. "I'm a shouter, Litvak, not a friggin' horse whisperer."

"You're definitely a shouter, Steckler. Don't think I didn't hear your 'Lithuania' last night. Where's your group, Steckler? Up ahead again, I suppose."

"Yes."

"First 'Lithuania,' then this horse shouting, and now you're alone again, Steckler. What am I going to do with you?"

"Leave me alone."

"You are alone, Steckler. That's the problem. You're alone without a permit."

He was out of the meadow and heading into the woods, following the creek. The toes of his boots moved along the dappled path. Heels followed. Who kisses the earth: toe or heel? Or both? A complete orgiastic step. Another.

"This Earth, this female form I walk and kiss. Am I approaching 'the madness amorous'? Have I sipped the 'mystic deliria'? If ever there was a time to, walk with me now, Walt!"

A hawk sprang from the underbrush and flew along the path in the tunnel between trees, a freshly caught ground squirrel in its talons. The squirrel's legs scissored the air frantically. Approaching Everett, the hawk banked and dropped its catch. The squirrel rolled when it landed, scurried up the trail, and was gone. The hawk perched on a pine branch, took one quick look down, lifted, and disappeared through the trees.

"And as to you death, and you bitter hug of mortality... it is idle to try to alarm me," Walt declaimed. "Stout as a horse, affectionate, haughty, electrical. I and this mystery here we stand." Middle of the trail, arms akimbo in his certainty, he stood with hat tilted rakishly.

"Wait a minute, Walt. What if the *bitter hug* comes as claws? I don't think that squirrel saw much *idle* about the experience. I expect he was mildly alarmed."

"The smallest sprout shows there is really no death."

"Which the smallest squirrel may not get, Walt."

"All goes onward and outward, nothing collapses,/ And to die is different from what any one supposed, and luckier."

"Can't buy that, Walt. You telling me that squirrel would be luckier dead? Is that what you're saying?"

"You'll figure it out," Walt said, strolling off in the same direction the lucky, or unlucky, squirrel had run, whistling loudly. With his walking stick, Everett tapped after him.

"What do you intend, Everett? A day with me, a day with her? A week with me, a week with her? A month with me, a month with her? A huge house, which you can't begin to afford, that would hold me, hold her, our children, her child? You say you love all of us, so you'll stable us together in one big barn?"

"There has to be a way. I just haven't found it yet."

"I should think you haven't *divined* it yet. You're going to need *godly* help to come up with anything I'd accept."

"We can be together. We can work this out, Laura."

"We can't."

"Why can't we?"

"Because I won't."

"And why won't you?"

"Because I can do better, Everett. I can do better."

Angling off the main trail, following the west side of the creek until he came to a shallow ford, Everett crossed at Colby Meadow. There wasn't a trail at this point, but others had crossed here. A track from the west side led into the creek. Footprints had worn a path up the opposite side.

Everett was taken aback that anyone crossed in this direction. "No one goes up McGee. It's my canyon."

Removing socks, feet back in boots, he waded in, water knee-deep. Crossing this second time, he didn't think of the cold as comforting. He was anxious to get on. Across the creek, he kept going, diagonally through the lower glade toward The Hermit. The upper end was a bog he kept to his left. Then he was on solid ground and clambered onto granite shelves at the meadow's edge. This was it, his night's camp. Soil had been smoothed between two pines for a tent site, a fire ring built in the clearing, but no one had camped recently. He was alone in Evolution Basin. Dropping his pack, he sat down, opening the front flap for his medication.

"I have arrived, Jonah. Colby Meadow. Still a fine spot."

He'd camped here with Jonah, with Laura, with Laura and Conrad, with Conrad. He missed the twelve-year-old Conrad he'd camped with here, but he didn't miss Conrad.

"You know," Conrad said, "you've been adrift since you left Mom. It's probably the worst damned decision you ever made in your life."

"I never left her. She drove me away."

"How could she not? After what you brought down?"

"After what I brought down? She asked me to go away."

"You left."

"Yes, I left. She drove me away."

"That's not quite the way I saw it. It appeared to me you left and never asked to be invited back."

"And what other fine things are quite the way you see them, Conrad?"

"Mom put her life back together; you didn't. You're still adrift. You've been adrift since you left her."

"Well, aren't we cheeky? Who do you think is keeping you in graduate school? Who's paying for that cool pint you've got your grubby fingers wrapped around? Someone who's pretty decently adrift if you ask me."

"You're generous, Dad. You've always been generous, but it doesn't change that since you left Mom, you've been fundamentally adrift."

"I think you're a little fucked up about adrift. Give me a break."

"That's you, Dad. You fuck things up, then ask for a break. I love you, but that's you."

"Was I really that bad, Conrad? Are you really that disappointed in me?"

The trees around him, the boulders, seemed gathered to hear testimony. The trees waited, the stones waited, Everett waited, but no one came forward, either to accuse or to vindicate. The slim sapling leaning toward the meadow was not Conrad, though Everett gazed at it a long time. The lodgepole bent over the granite was not Laura, though Everett focused on it too a long time. Each boulder and tree seemed poised for him to ferret a memory out of it. He felt he was abandoning them, but didn't want the memories, the fitful anamnesis of acts and places and sorrows terribly haunting and deceiving precisely because they were fragmentary and fleeting. No, he would not look at rock nor tree again except as form: crystal inside rock, cell inside wood. Structure and function only, not association. Only the abstract—that which is not open to change or chance.

He stared at the dirt between his feet, then the short trodden grasses past his feet, then the dark shadow of a tall pine leaning into the clearing, then the rust-hued grass of the meadow. The pools of the creek were tinged pastel from the alpenglow on the crest behind him. The peak of Mt. Darwin glowed pale orange and rose-tinted when he turned to look. Streamers of sunlight hovered above the canyon. Boulders in the upper meadow—each surrounded by a collar of willow brush—glowed luminous in the twilight.

"I've never been able to hold tight the abstract, Jonah. You always told me beauty enhances but does not sustain. I believed you, and I believe you now, but it's hard not to believe too—here, tonight, in this meadow, under these mountains, on this earth—that beauty suffices even if it does not sustain. We ought to accept what we're given if it suffices, ought we not? This is what I have come to believe, Jonah. This is what I have come to accept."

XI

"What wonders saw Whitman when he lay dying?" Everett pondered, eyes open middle of night, sky full of stars, tips of pine trees framing his view.

Inside his sick room—friends in chairs round his bed, walls covered in rose-patterned paper, dark armoire in the corner, mirror on the wall beside the window, thick woven curtains open, window shut to keep vapors out—Whitman whispers, "Shift, Warry," asking to be turned. His last words. But what saw he in his poet's eye? Horseman riding toward him with wild-flapping pennants? Orchestra whirling him away, music receding beyond his ardors? "Ever the sobbing liquid of life." Ever? Was a goblet proffered for his thirst that final moment? Was death residuum in the cup? "Ever the trestles of death." Was there a beam to hang from forever? Surely death didn't come as the poet foresaw it. Surely it did not arrive as a phrase, an image, a whisper of air, even for someone who called it *luckier.*

"Was it luckier, Walt? Was it?"

The friends in chairs get up and go out; walkers on streets outside continue their steps; the farmer plows to the end of his furrow, turns his team, plows another. Seeds dropped into the furrow sprout; the earth lives. The six to seven thousand stars the eye naked and unadorned can perceive—the same stars Whitman looked at, that Copernicus could have, that Aristotle could have—live. Life beyond imagination. A hundred billion stars in the Milky Way, ten trillion galaxies in the universe with their hundred billion stars each. Numbers unfathomable to persuade us there is nothing but life, nothing but light, and still we are not convinced. Jonah was right. These are numbers only, these are least things; these we will let go, with the wars, the histories, the critical patterns of human development and strife; these we will let go inevitably to focus on our own puny, quivering flame as it weakens, then ceases. We pare our perceptions to approach this nothingness. We whittle our needs to "Shift, Warry."

The squirrel dropped by the hawk that morning might be lying awake too, might be alone under those six to seven thousand stars, might be facing death under a Milky Way of a hundred billion stars. Surely the hawk's talons had torn hair and flesh. Or was the squirrel uninjured, dropped to live another day, asleep in its nest, unmindful of the hawk, unmindful of the human, unmindful of the stars? Awaiting dawn, but sleeping, while Everett waited wide eyed.

"What, could ye not watch with me for one hour?"

"Take this cup away from me," the old priest would recite precisely, as if fearful he might get words out of order, then pause and let his eyes roam across the catechism class. "This is the incredible moment in our faith," he would go on. "This is the moment where for a moment the son of God becomes man, wholly man, crying out in fear to let this cup pass. In that moment he is all of us, all our fears, all our uncertainties." He'd tremble ever so slightly, holding himself just below rapture, face lifted, wisps of uncombed hair almost vibrating, sometimes tearing up but never allowing himself to weep. "In those words is the mystery of our faith. God made man, pleading, 'Take this cup away from me.' God for that fleeting moment becomes wholly man."

There was no mystery for Everett; he'd never got within light years of the faith the old priest was so infused with. Homilies were simply tales to him, stories put together as a barrier against death, the human fear to step forward into the unknowable. And surely to fear the unknown is a lack of trust in the Son of God. Could not a believer be called into account for that? If there were a Caller, if one of those distant stars were the Son of Man on his way back, headlight beaming, flight pattern established, time of arrival fixed? If only, yes, but for the time being, the unknowable abideth. Did not the prophets say so? And the earth abideth, and the stars and the darkness abideth, and the bother with the night is that it's long.

But "The sun also ariseth, and the sun goeth down, and hasteth to his place where he arose." Everett imagined the sun speeding around the planet, trailing sunlight like a scarf, crossing the Atlantic but still well hidden behind the planet, hastening to whatever place the ancient prophet had so sought to have it rise from.

Darkness was still latched firmly over the landscape. From his sleeping bag he could see his food bag hanging from the branch where he'd tied it, perfectly still, dark silhouette against stars and sky. He'd focus on it until he could really see. Then it would be dawn. Far better to pass the night mindlessly watching his food stash than to lie awake thinking of an old priest, a lost faith, and a verse written in a dark mood. "For in much wisdom is much grief, and he that increaseth knowledge increaseth sorrow."

XII

Lamarck, Mendel, Darwin. Peaks golden in morning sunlight, light spilling down rock spires into forest. The creek glides lazily into the meadow, funneling water between grassy banks. A narrow, knife-blade flow slips out of each pool and the creek snakes on. Sunlight follows the water, gilding the tips of grasses flaxen. Everett watches all from his promontory, moves only to find his medications, lifts his head to swallow tablets and water. He sets the water bottle down, lowers his head to watch again.

Beauty, not time, is part of the fundamental structure of the universe, beauty that lives in earth, fire, water—the cosmic winch that pulls sunlight across a clearing. Or does beauty require at least the concept of time? If the light came at once and burst over the meadow, would it be as beguiling? Does time enhance beauty, suffusing the sunrise in its slow progression with a splendor the lightning bolt in its abruptness cannot attain? Or are both fundamental and unable to be perceived separately? He allowed these questions to form, then let them drift away, to float skyward and dissipate in the bright sunlight until he looked out only on grass and meadow, water and creek, rock and mountain, sky and earth; then looked out only on grass, water, rock, sky; then just looked.

Eventually he slipped out of his sleeping bag. He strolled down the outcrop and across the upper meadow to the creek where he dipped water and drank, then sat on a sandbar. Upstream roots of alder bushes turned the shallow flow toward the opposite bank, against which it bumped and came back toward him, surface overlapping itself in continuous riffles—sky mirrored in each—as gravel on the stream's bottom slowed the water. The stream edged against the sandbar and flowed on. As Everett watched ripples form and fade, he felt a heightened contentment. Impassive, soothing.

"'And he shewed me a pure river of water of life.' And I, Everett, saw these things." What was there in revelation that the earth had not always shown?

Late in the morning, he broke camp, following the outcrop on which he'd slept toward McGee Lakes. There was no marked trail. Occasionally there were cairns hikers had built, but mostly he walked through stands of lodgepole in which no sign of human passage was evident. He followed the slope of the hill, climbing, pausing often, reminding himself he had no goal for the day. A mile out of Colby Meadow he crossed a feeder stream coming down from his right and stopped where it twisted through a small grove and disappeared toward McGee Creek. Looking back, he could see a segment of the meadow far below. He was surprised, pleased he'd climbed so quickly.

He rested an hour before he went on, angling uphill. The slope he followed paralleled McGee Creek. Another feeder stream meandered through a flat he was crossing. He stopped and surveyed it, then turned to follow and explore it. In fifty yards the forest ended where a granite wall began. Broken logs had tumbled off the wall and lay piled along its base.

It took most of the afternoon for him to set up camp. Next to a large log, he cleared an area to spread his sleeping pad and bag. He gathered small poles and branches and laid them against the log to build a lean-to. Most of the structure was bare sticks, but he dragged two larger branches over, twigs and drying needles still attached, and placed them on top. The structure looked more like a brush pile than a shelter, which suited him.

In a sandy fan at the base of a boulder not far from his lean-to, he cleared a circle for fire. He gathered firewood, choosing smaller dry sticks that would burn hot and quick. With pine needles and twigs he built a starter teepee, stacked firewood near it. Removing his food, he sorted out a piece of cheese, a few dried apricots, half a bittersweet chocolate bar, then carried the remainder into the brush and scattered it.

Back at his gear, he lifted out of a side pocket a pitch-lined bota bag he had not touched yet this trip. Opening it, he sniffed the stopper, breathing deeply. He took a mouthful, holding it for a long moment. Fine California brandy, Mendocino County, alembic distilled, aged seven years. He lay on the rock in the early evening, sipping brandy, nibbling cheese, apricots, chocolate.

He'd returned from a week in Utah, a trip to audit an airbag initiator subcontractor. Friday night he took Josie to dinner. She was stunning, red hair dropping onto her shoulders, eyes bright and arresting. Everett told stories of how the lead engineer in Utah called him *A California Auditor* and questioned every finding and correction he insisted on. Josie laughed, and he was enchanted with her laughter, but there was something not quite right, he realized, something that wasn't about the dinner or the conversation or the cognac they sipped after the meal.

"What is it?" he finally asked.

"I don't know if we should talk about it here."

"Why not? I can take it."

"I need to be by myself, Everett. I need a new life different from the life I had when I was raped. I need not to see you now. I need to go on by myself."

"Are you getting rid of Teddy too?"

"Don't be beastly, Everett, please. You know I won't get rid of Teddy. But I do need a new life for the woman I am, a completely new start to become the woman I have to be. I know this hurts, Everett. I'm sorry," she said, reaching across the table for his hands, squeezing them.

He imagined himself alone on the Greenland icecap, screaming, icebergs calving around him. He allowed her to hold his hands and waited.

"It's not just having you in the house and sleeping with you," she said. "I need to not have contact. I need to be by myself absolutely."

"How long will this be?"

"I don't know."

"Will I be allowed to check in from time to time?"

"I don't think that works. I need a complete separation, Everett. I need to start a completely new life."

"A completely new life, Jonah. Imagine that. You could have used one. I could right now. We should have started a business of new lives, new starts, new vistas, not old philosophies and old poems and believing there was wisdom in the old that could tell us something about the now and the still-to-be-imagined. What did I care for the still-to-be-imagined? I wanted Josie. I did not get her. My heart was grieved, but not embittered. And that allowed me to believe in some small way I held on to a gift that had slipped through my fingers. The unembittered heart I kept, Jonah. I have it with me now."

Shadows spread over the mountains; a band of sunlight retreated up the peaks. Everett lit the fire teepee and watched wisps of smoke rise through the sticks. He lay near the fire, feeding it patiently, one kindling piece at a time, watching flames devour each, laying another in the embers of the one before. When it was fully dark, he roused himself and pulled his pack toward the fire.

He took out all medications and washed down two Oxycontin with sips of brandy, stuffing the remaining pills loose into his jacket pocket. He tossed the pill pouch on the fire, where it flamed up and burned, then lay on his side and fought his way through nausea. Stars pulsed, spun, fragmented, spiraling toward him like celestial darts. He turned from them, closed his eyes, waited—and when the queasiness passed, went back to his pack. Taking out the line he'd used for hanging food, he coiled it and threw it on the fire. Next the food bag. He put his reading packet aside, and used the biodegradable knife to slit the pack into quarters. Tossing each on the fire, he waited for one to burn, then tossed another. When they were gone, he set the knife on the fire and watched flames run across the blade and devour it. Stoking the fire with another piece of wood, he picked up the reading packet.

He burned Ecclesiastes first, which seemed right. Surely the sun understood its comings and goings by now without need of text. The paper curled on itself in the fire, bits of ash floating away. The pages from the history of the Nez Perce he burned next, then essays by Maclean, James and Kant, stories by Bierce and Faulkner, what remained of Shakespeare gnawed by mice. He tore pages out one at a time, looked at each as if to read it one more time, but just looked, pattern of word on sheet, then laid it on the fire; flames edged through and consumed what had been written and printed.

Last came the poets. "September 1, 1939," went up in flames. Villon, Kinnell, and Leonard Cohen, until he was left with Whitman, Yeats, Stevens. He fingered the pages that held their poems, reluctant to let them go, finally choosing Whitman, holding each page in both hands like a priest lifting the Eucharist before placing it on the fire. "Every atom" consumed away, “the smoke of my own breath,” “the belch'd words … loos'd to the eddies of the wind.” Had the poet written these lines to be burned? Intent fulfilled. The pages of Whitman were gone.

Yeats and Stevens remained. As concession to Jonah, he'd hold Stevens last. So the “Circus Animal” burned, “Anne Gregory,” “Byzantium,” “School Children” “with sixty or more winters” on their heads. “When You Are Old and Gray” burned, leaving love no chance to flee, the flames taking it, no option here “to hide his face amid a crowd of stars.” Was love exposed in burning Yeats? No matter. “Beauty dies of beauty, worth of worth.”

Surely Stevens was a strange choice for last, but the mind of winter had intrigued Jonah, perhaps—for him—the necessary mien to face death. “No one faces death boldly,” Jonah said. “In battle, perhaps the warrior faces the event fearlessly, but never the actual dying. You wonder if I am fearful. I am.” So not without fear, not boldly, Jonah passed his last days, a mind of winter the talisman he carried out of life. Everett lit the page at a small flame and watched the poem disappear from bottom up: “the listener in the snow,” “the misery in the sound of the wind,” “the junipers shagged with ice,” until only “mind of winter” remained when he dropped it in the fire.

The brandy was gone. He shook the bota bag close to his ear to be sure, before tossing the goatskin on the fire. It flared up, lighting up the scrub conifers and rock, glowed for a moment, and faded. Everett lit a candle and sat by the fire, shivering as it burned down, sometimes glancing at stars, more often gazing fixedly at the waning embers. When he could see no light in the fire, he poured half his water over it, dribbling a circle around the pile of cinders. Steam rose and ash scattered. Then the embers were still.

Getting up was hard, but he pushed himself to his feet. He carried the candle and water bottle and shuffled to his sleeping bag. Dripping a wax base, he anchored the candle on the ground nearby. He was cold, shaking wildly as he worked himself into the bag. For a long time he fought fainting. When he was steady, he found the pills in his jacket pocket and swallowed six with water, and this time was sick, really sick. Not allowing himself to vomit, he twisted chin down hard, bit his lips to keep them closed. Recovering slightly, he turned on his back and nudged the larger poles above him. They slid down the log, sticks and brush settling over him. He could sense their weight on his ribcage and face but could not feel their shapes.

The candle burned out.

He lay with hands spread on his chest, motionless, fingers interlaced. Wasn't getting much oxygen. Maybe it was the mountain air. Maybe he had stopped breathing. His shoulders tingled, then the tingle ran along his arms and out through his fingertips.

In gaps between sticks, Everett looked up at stars, billions of bits of light falling toward Earth, beating against the planet. Starlight bounced off the granite around him, ricocheting crazily. The earth was a mirror sending waves rebounding into space, the light of a dead star boomeranging toward a source no longer there, so flinging itself onward forever. He could feel himself lifting away, soaring at breakneck speed with these orphaned waves—past billions of galaxies, billions of stars—until there was darkness only, and still they sped on, ever into darkness, ever into space.

Made in the USA
Lexington, KY
24 October 2019

55831928R00100

FICTION

Brothers and sisters drawn by their father's death back home to the family farm, a friend wrestling with the ghastly consequences of his own inattention, a very-ill man's pilgrimage to the high mountains of California—these spare and deeply western stories crackle with hard-earned grief, love, and, when it matters most, humor.

Daniel Duane, author of *Lighting Out* and *Caught Inside*

This cleanly and powerfully written collection puts one in mind of certain eminent writers of the West – Wallace Stegner, David Vann, and the Kerouac of *Dharma Bums* – forming, unlike many story collections, a unity of mood and theme, and putting on display some high-level literary chops. Mr. Schwartz feels strongly and the storms of emotion in his stories lead to deep skies.

Robert Roper, author of *Nabokov in America: On the Road to Lolita*, and *Fatal Mountaineer: The High-Altitude Life and Death of Will Unsoeld*

Ben Schwartz lives in Northern California with his wife and two children.
His website is: https://bgschwartz.com

ISBN 9780989127776